WRITTEN BY

BEN ACKER & BEN BLACKER

ILLUSTRATED BY

ANNIE WU

DISNEP
LUCASFILM
PRESS

LOS ANGELES · NEW YORK

For information address Disney • Lucasfilm Press,
1101 Flower Street, Glendale, California 91201.

Printed in the United States of America

First Hardcover Edition, October 2017

1 3 5 7 9 10 8 6 4 2

FAC-020093-17234

ISBN 978-1-4847-0498-1

Library of Congress Control Number on file

Reinforced binding

Designed by Jason Wojtowicz

Visit the official *Star Wars* website at: www.starwars.com.

SUSTAINABLE FORESTRY INITIATIVE   Certified Sourcing
www.sfiprogram.org
SFI-00993

THIS LABEL APPLIES TO TEXT STOCK

This book was begun shortly after we lost Carrie Fisher, and her wit, strength, and humor in dark times loom large over it. Acker & Blacker wish to dedicate this book to Carrie, Mark Hamill, Harrison Ford, Kenny Baker, Anthony Daniels, Peter Mayhew, George Lucas, and everyone who created the playground in which we now get to play. As well as to J. J., Rian, and all of the people inspiring us in that playground.

CHAPTER

01

MATTIS WAS THINKING about General Leia.

He'd seen her across the command center, rushing from room to room at the Resistance base or giving orders or listening to intelligence briefings. She embodied determination and the wisdom that comes from integrity as she decided the best course of action for the Resistance. For the galaxy.

Mattis knew the stories of Leia Organa before she was the experienced and judicious military leader of the Resistance against the First Order. Mattis collected stories of the old days in the way that other kids collected grav-ball badges. He was hooked by tales of the fight against the Empire. He found inspiration in those old stories. He found guidance. He also found heroes.

Leia Organa had been a princess, a captive, a senator, and a freedom fighter. She was imprisoned by the Empire and enslaved by a Hutt, had seen the love of her life frozen in carbonite and her home planet destroyed. But that woman, whom Mattis saw calmly command and thoughtfully lead, taught him to never give up.

And somehow, even with all she had endured, even as she fought and strategized and inspired—all very serious business—Leia was funny. When J-Squadron had accidentally shut off the power in the compound just as the pilots returned and it took everything everyone had to bring them in safely, Mattis was convinced he was going to be drummed out. While they had awaited their punishment in Admiral Ackbar's office, General Leia had come in and looked them over.

"You're responsible for the power outage?" she asked.

"We're the screwups, yes, ma'am," Dec answered with uncharacteristic deference.

"Some of my best friends are screwups," she said with a smirk. "We need more screwups around here." She'd left them feeling better for the moment. How easy would it have been for her to become embittered? How sad but understandable for her to lose her fire and grow stern and cruel? Leia never did. Mattis hoped he'd retain his sense of humor through his current perilous circumstances as a prisoner of the First Order, alone in a damp cell on the swamp planet of Vodran. Assuming, of course, he got out alive and had been funny in the first place.

Mattis wasn't the kind of kid to get discouraged. Even though he had faced a series of calamitous events since he'd joined the Resistance, and even though those events, one after another, had led him to the cell on Vodran, Mattis remained optimistic. He'd joined the Resistance for a reason. This was part of it.

He wanted to make a difference. That was why he'd left the orphan farm on Durkteel. It was Mattis's destiny, he knew, to bring about change in the galaxy. He would become a hero like Leia Organa or Admiral Ackbar. For what other reason had he been imbued with the Force, the arcane energy that was created by and bound together all living things? The Force was what made Mattis special. It was what made him want to do more than just harvest hemmel on Durkteel. And though the Force hadn't yet manifested itself in him, he knew it would emerge when the time was right. It was why, even now, sitting alone on the cold hard floor of his cold hard cell, he didn't overly worry. The Force was within him somewhere.

Of course, the Force hadn't been much help in keeping him out of this catastrophe and all the catastrophes that led up to this one. There had been plenty of opportunities along the way for the Force to intervene. When Mattis arrived on the Resistance base and befriended AG-90, a droid with a singular personality who looked cobbled together from junkyard components, the Force might have said "Watch out, buddy." The Force could have cleared its throat in warning when AG introduced Mattis to the droid's "brother," Dec Hansen, who was charming enough to talk them all into trouble and only sometimes out of it. Or when Dec suggested that, for a laugh, they hack the base's mainframe. That the true reason for this transgression was benign made little difference. Admiral Ackbar came down hard on Mattis and his new friends. The Force had nothing to say about any of that before, during, or after. It did nothing to keep Mattis out of hot water at any step. If that wasn't how the Force worked, it was how it *should* work, in Mattis's opinion.

It had been a torpedo to blazes since then. Admiral Ackbar placed Mattis, Dec, AG, and their friends, a bookish behemoth named Sari Nadle and a hyperactive Rodian named Klimo, under the rigid instruction of a human rule book called Jo Jerjerrod and his brusque Zeltron second-in-command, Lorica Demaris. AG caught Jo communicating with the First Order and assumed Jo was spying on the Resistance. The spite between them came to a head when Jo tried to reset AG-90, whose peculiar personality was due to the fact that his memory had never been wiped since the day Dec's mom built him.

The fracas had culminated in all of J-Squadron being sent to do scrapping work on Vodran, a murky, humid planet on the Outer Rim. Vodran was a monster-beset swampland once occupied by a nasty, imperious Hutt. The atmosphere on Vodran was so muggy and stifling that Mattis felt he could cut it with a dull blade. The humidity irritated everyone, setting them against each other. The Resistance was not the place of harmonious camaraderie Mattis had thought it would be. Until it was.

It took an animal attack—really, multiple attacks by many animals—before J-Squadron pulled together. It was the incident with the sarlacc pit that started it. Each squadron member—Mattis, Dec, AG, Sari, Jo, Lorica, and Klimo—had a hand in rescuing someone from that pit. After the harrowing incident with the sarlacc, Mattis felt he'd found the fellowship he'd expected from the Resistance. It was then that Dec confronted Jo about his presumed treachery. Jo revealed he had secretly joined the Resistance under the noses of his First Order officer parents. He wasn't a traitor to his squad mates, but to his family. Mattis felt they understood one another, or at least they were starting to. Then their group was torn apart.

First by a rolling pack of snarling, stupid tawds, followed by a cadre of vicious rancors. Dec and Sari escaped in one of their short-range shuttles. Klimo commandeered the other one, and he was poised to rescue the rest of them, but he never made it. The last image Mattis had of his Rodian friend was of Klimo in the cockpit of the shuttle, struggling to maintain its lift against rancor after rancor, until finally the struggle ended tragically. Mattis felt horrible, and worse, he felt responsible.

Klimo was the first recruit Mattis had met on the transport to the Resistance base. He was wiry and sunny, always fidgeting, and restless for adventure. Mattis could only wonder what might have become of Klimo if they hadn't befriended one another. Klimo might have been warm and safe now, bouncing like a rathtar after three cups of caf back in his bunk on the base. Mattis knew it was unhelpful to his present situation to think that way—a guilty conscience wouldn't free him from this mess—but it was difficult not to. So, again, he thought of General Leia. Mattis was certain the general felt guilt about the death and chaos she'd had a hand in, but he was equally sure that she didn't dwell upon it for too long. Based on the stories, he figured she would use that guilt, that anger, that sense of justice to fuel her crusade. She could transform those negative feelings into positive action; that was what made her a hero. He would do the same, and that would make him the hero he knew he was. Maybe that'd wake the Force within him.

When that happened, Mattis was confident it

would feel like the rush of riding the speeder bike that had zoomed him away from the creatures on Vodran. He was confident it would *not* feel like he felt now, after escaping the deadly fauna but ending up surrounded by First Order stormtroopers.

The moment before J-Squadron was surrounded, they'd dismounted the speeder bikes on tall, wet grass. Mattis and Lorica stretched and caught their breaths. Jo had his back turned, measuring how far they'd ridden. AG checked his speeder's gauge, flicking it back and forth, making a sharp *clack-clack* sound.

"All of you, freeze where you are."

Mattis didn't know which of the storm-troopers, suddenly all around them, had spoken. Mattis neither fainted (which he nearly did) nor came unglued (which is what he wanted to do). Maybe he was too physically and mentally spent, or maybe his brain just refused to believe that he had fought against and hid and fled in the muck and mud and brush from wild animals and his own friends only to fall into the hands of a real evil enemy who wanted to do much worse than eat him or annoy him.

The First Order had emerged shortly after

General Leia had left the New Republic to start the Resistance, and was increasingly a threat to the galaxy. At least, it was according to General Leia and those who believed her. Mattis believed her. The First Order could not be trusted, and recently, there had been murmurs that the group was planning something terrible.

The stormtroopers closed the circle around them.

"What do we do?" Mattis whispered.

Lorica, rigid and still, hissed, "Freeze." Jo had his hands up, palms facing outward. He was frozen, too. AG scratched his chin as if he were capable of itching. He leaned in to get a good look at the speeder bike gauge as it continued to clack defiantly.

"Stop doing that," one of the stormtroopers said. Then, to Jo, "Tell your droid to stop doing that."

"What am I doing?" AG asked.

Mattis tried to catch AG's attention. "Aygee, don't."

"I gotta check this gauge, though, man," AG drawled to the stormtrooper nearest him.

"Don't call the stormtroopers 'man,' Aygee," Jo sneered.

"That's on me," AG replied, raising a hand in innocence, continuing to flip the gauge with a hypnotic click. "I can be thoughtless sometimes. Too casual, I'm told." As he spoke, AG climbed back astride the speeder bike, clacking the gauge.

"Stop what you're doing!" a stormtrooper barked.

Mattis whispered sharply to Lorica, "He's going to get killed."

"Evasive. Maneuvers. On my signal," Lorica whispered carefully.

AG nodded, but it looked like a shudder if you didn't know AG.

"Don't," Jo whispered even more carefully than Lorica had.

Mattis couldn't believe any of this. There were about a dozen stormtroopers, all armed, and AG and Lorica wanted to make a run for it? They were crazier than a pair of wampas vacationing on Tatooine!

"Move off that speeder," the same stormtrooper commanded AG. The angry stormtrooper had one violently scratched lens, as if a small clawed creature had tried to enter his right eye.

"Okay, let me just . . ." AG trailed off. Then he gunned the engine!

"Now!" Lorica growled, and took off running.

Jo continued to stand calmly with his hands raised. Mattis tensed, unsure if Jo was about to run, too. Mattis felt the stormtroopers' eyes on him as if it were his turn to decide, which terrified him enough that he took off after Lorica as best he could. She had a big lead and had always been better than he was at running and pretty much everything else. Blaster fire pelted the ground around them. The stormtroopers chasing them through the muck were lousy shots and needed the practice they were getting from shooting at Mattis and Lorica. But the practice was working, as some of them were getting pretty close. Mattis dove face-first into the mud as a shot stung his heel. Smoke came off his boot.

Before he could push himself up again, he was grabbed and lifted fiercely to his feet. His left heel, where the shot had fried his boot, burned. He howled in pain.

"Stop that racket," the stormtrooper said.

"You're hurting me," Mattis replied.

"You'll get more once we get to the detention center."

Mattis tried to think of something cutting he might say to deflate the stormtrooper's venom, but he was too afraid. The other stormtroopers watched Lorica run away through the swamp. The terrain was too dangerous to keep up the chase. If only Mattis had made it a little farther.

The stormtrooper who'd spoken before motioned to Lorica's shrinking figure in the near distance. "Can you take her out?" he asked his nearby cohort.

"I got her," the other stormtrooper said, lifting his blaster rifle to his eye.

Mattis struggled and screamed as loud as he could, "Lorica!" Without turning, she dropped into some reeds and disappeared.

The trooper holding Mattis tossed him into the mud. "You," he said to the stormtrooper who still had his rifle poised to shoot. "Keep watch. That grass moves, shoot it. She shows her pink head, shoot it."

Lorica's bright skin would be hard to miss against the green and brown of the wet meadow. "Come back in!" Mattis shouted, standing unsteadily. "They'll kill you if you don't!" He hoped that they wouldn't kill her either way. The stormtroopers hadn't killed him yet, so he held out hope.

Everyone waited and nothing happened.

"We'll kill *you* if she doesn't," the mean trooper said. "Tell her that."

Words died in Mattis's throat.

"They're threatening me," he croaked.

The stormtroopers pointed their guns at where Lorica had been. Thoughts churned in Mattis's mind. He thought faster than he ever had before.

"If you come back now, they won't shoot," he yelled. "Look, they're lowering their guns." He looked pleadingly at the stormtroopers, who made a great sarcastic show of lowering their guns.

Slowly, Lorica's head rose from the reeds. He could tell, even at this distance, that she was furious at having to surrender.

The stormtroopers were rougher with Lorica than they'd been with Mattis, probably galled that she'd made them trudge through so much muck. Their nice white armor was splattered. A small victory, but Mattis would take it. The stormtroopers escorted Mattis and Lorica back to where Jo remained, with his hands now touching the top of his head. He still wore that smug, mild expression. The troopers tossed Lorica and Mattis into the mud beside Jo. Two others dragged AG-90, whose head was cocked at an upsetting, disjointed angle, into their circle.

"My name is Jo Jerjerrod," Jo told them in a tone that informed Mattis this wasn't his first time repeating the words in order to command respect and curry favor. "I am the son of Jul and Jax Jerjerrod of the First Order Security Bureau. I demand to speak to your commanding officer."

The lead stormtrooper—the one who'd roughed up Mattis, then Lorica—sighed through his helmet comlink. It sounded like static, but his or her impatience was clear.

"You're *all* going to see Commander Wanten. Just get marching."

With that, the stormtroopers herded Mattis, Lorica, Jo, and AG into a small cluster, and they shuffled along through the mud in silence. Because of his skewed head, AG kept straying carelessly from the group, but their minders would curb the droid's wandering, shoving him roughly back into the pack.

As they crested a spongy hummock, a palace was revealed beyond and below it. Wood-and-metal fencing surrounded a good portion of the land around the palace, which must have belonged to Harra the Hutt, the galactic gangster who'd claimed Vodran before the First Order ran her out. The palace wasn't large, though a turret reached crookedly into the sky, giving it height. There was a blown-out section of the palace's far wall, where the First Order stormtroopers must have made their initial advance. Two rows of smaller structures framed the near side of the palace. Every structure was slick with condensation. Black moss invaded the buildings in ugly splotches.

Mattis's knees gave out, and he dipped into the muddy hummock. Lorica grabbed him and pulled him upright again.

"Thanks."

"Welcome to our new home," she said dryly.

Mattis didn't know how much time had passed since then. It felt like days, but it was probably only hours. The stormtroopers had separated them upon arrival at the palace gates. The last thing Mattis saw of his friends was Jo being led into the palace proper while the rest of them were hustled toward the row of structures alongside.

Those complexes were divided into small cells. As the stormtroopers ushered him down the corridor, Mattis saw that some of the cells had bunks built into them, while others contained just nests of patchy blankets on the floor. One of their escorts peeled off from the group and took Lorica roughly with him. She didn't speak to Mattis as he jerked his head back to watch her go; she nodded, though, and he thought that was a good sign. He suspected she was already planning an escape. Hopefully, she wouldn't do anything too impulsive. Hopefully, she would take him with her.

A moment later, another stormtrooper, the one with the scratched lens, grabbed AG and hauled him down a connecting corridor. As he left, he told his cohort, "Put this one on ice in cell four."

Mattis had little idea what being "put on ice" might entail and didn't relish finding out, but his escort nodded and continued marching him down the corridor. When they were near the end, the stormtrooper punched some symbols on a keypad and an old-fashioned metal cage door slid open. He shoved Mattis inside. There was nothing in the cell except for a stool.

"Sit," the stormtrooper said. Mattis sat. "Stay," the stormtrooper commanded. Mattis stayed. Where else would he go? The stormtrooper had punched the cage door closed, so Mattis was trapped.

It was when so much time had passed that Mattis figured he'd been forgotten that he started thinking about General Leia. What would she do in his position? From the stories, Mattis knew she'd been captured at least once by the Empire. She'd faced more pain, more difficulty, more distress than he was presently. Mattis looked at the ceiling—gray, damp, cracked—he looked at the floor—damp, gray, cracked—and he took in each wall—cracked, damp, gray—just as he'd done mechanically for the past hour. Hours. Who knew how long?

As soon as that first stormtrooper had left, Mattis had inspected the cell. The walls were cracked, yes, but it would have taken a very large tool to bust through them. There were no windows. He was stuck.

Mattis could hear General Leia and Admiral Ackbar talking about him. Their words were indistinct. It sounded like Leia asked if she could open the door, and Admiral Ackbar said no, that Mattis was a trap. Leia disagreed and the door slid open with a screeching complaint, and Mattis woke, startled. He was slumped in the corner of the cell; he'd fallen asleep. Of course General Leia and Admiral Ackbar weren't there. He'd been alone, captured, trapped. Alone until now, anyway.

A thick-trunked bald man in a First Order uniform stood in the cell doorway, staring with beady blue eyes at Mattis. He appeared to have once been athletic, but now the muscle had turned to fat that hung from his body in fleshy pillows. The man didn't seem happy about that. He didn't seem happy about anything. Mattis didn't feel any need to try to change the man's feelings.

The man wiped at the wave of sweat that crested on his brow and said, "What's your name?"

Mattis didn't speak, just continued to sit in the corner of the room. The pillowy man shook his head as if to say, *So this is how it's going to be?* Well, it was, Mattis thought in response. This was exactly how it would be. Mattis and his friends were too new to the Resistance to have been taught capture protocol, but he was smart enough to keep quiet. It wouldn't help anyone for Mattis to run his mouth, though his every instinct was telling him to do just that. He couldn't help it. Babbling was his default response to overwhelming fear. But he thought about Lorica and the fierce look she'd have given him if she were there, so he kept his mouth shut.

The man let out a heavy, phlegmy sigh, as if the heat were pressing down on his chest. He pulled the stool closer to him. It screeched against the concrete floor. Mattis worried that if the man sat on it, the stool might break. The man seemed to think of this at the same moment and just rested a beefy hand on it and leaned on that.

"My name is Wanten. This"—he motioned vaguely all around him—"this is my place. It's a detention center for the First Order *of* the first order." The man paused, then added, "Rather, it will be. That's my joke. When something is 'of the first order' it means that it is of a very high quality. As you can see, this detention center is not yet of a very high quality. But it will be."

"It's a bad start," Mattis said. He couldn't help himself. It made him feel a bit better to be insolent to this First Order chump.

Wanten pursed his lips in a kind of meaty smile. It was more unsettling than the frown. "You have a sense of humor," Wanten said. "That's good. A sense of humor will be necessary in this detention center." He sidestepped the stool so that he could rest his other hand on it. "This room you are in is called the Bad Place. You do not want to be in here."

Mattis looked around. The room was pretty bad; he already knew that. But if this was the Bad Place, then it stood to reason there might be better places in the detention center. When he sensed Wanten watching him do that calculation, Mattis studied the floor again.

"Yes," Wanten continued, "there are better places. We have knocked down walls so that there are rooms larger than this, with beds and even blankets and sinks. You'll see. You'll be taken to one"—Mattis allowed himself a moment of hope before Wanten swept it away by saying—"if you cooperate."

"Cooperate how?" Mattis asked, not intending to cooperate in the least.

"You'll find that cooperation will afford you any number of perks and luxuries. Not just beds and blankets but time to exercise your skinny legs in the Fold."

It took Mattis a moment to realize that the Fold was a place—a penned-in outdoor area where the mud had been scraped away or layered over with dirty, scratchy turf. He'd seen it as he was led from the palace gates to these barracks. It didn't seem like a place he'd want to exercise or even spend much time at all, but it was, Mattis supposed, preferable to these dank, do-nothing cells.

"I would like to send you to the Fold. I would. But you need to give me a reason."

Mattis stared at the floor.

"You'll tell us everything you know about the terrorist group calling itself the Resistance," Wanten said. "In return"—he made that unnerving grimace-smile again and opened his hands as if welcoming Mattis to his new home, which, in a way, he was—"you'll have so many comforts. You won't believe how many. Doesn't that sound nice?"

Mattis shrugged.

Wanten sighed in a show of great false patience. "You're young and don't seem very able. Your knowledge, I suspect, is limited." Wanten folded his hands together like a priest. "I don't mean this as an insult. I mean to say that you don't need to be afraid to divulge anything you know, because the breadth of what you know is really so narrow. I suspect that anything you tell me will only be *so* helpful." On the word *so*, Wanten held his finger and thumb a few centimeters apart. "So you should feel agreeable to declare anything you know. Do you feel agreeable?"

Wanten then rested both of his loaf-sized hands on the stool, which buckled but didn't break. He waited for Mattis to respond. Sweat glistened on the man's thick scalp.

That was when Mattis felt what General Leia must have felt when she was captured by the Empire so long ago. Inadvertently, Wanten had shown Mattis a way to stay alive on Vodran, as well as Mattis's own worth. This man, Wanten, was desperate for information, which made sense. A half-constructed detention center on a swamp planet was hardly the place for the First Order's most elite officer. Wanten was, at best, a person with a small sphere of power who wanted more. It stood to reason that Wanten wouldn't do anything too drastic to Mattis until Mattis gave him information that would put Wanten in his superiors' charitable regard. And while he strung Wanten along, Mattis would catalogue details about *this* place, this place that the Resistance knew nothing about; if they had, certainly Admiral Ackbar wouldn't have sent Mattis and his friends there. Mattis would endure whatever pain and torture Wanten brought upon him because, like Leia before him, Mattis now possessed that which the First Order could never extinguish.

Mattis had hope.

Wanten was quiet for a long time but for his mucousy breathing. When it became clear to him that Mattis wasn't going to share any information, he stood up straight. Wanten was surprisingly tall.

"Fine, fine," he said, still in that falsely friendly yet heartless tone. "You don't need to tell me anything. After all, you weren't taken alone, were you?"

Mattis went lightheaded.

"Your friend, the girl, maybe she'll talk. Alternatively, it's easy to make a droid tell his master things. And I could easily become his master. And of course, there's always the Jerjerrod boy," Wanten said. "He's already told me all about his time in the Resistance. Did you know your friend has been a spy for the First Order all of this time? Probably not. He's a good boy, trustworthy. I'm sure you trusted him. I'm sure that everyone in the Resistance did. And he will tell us everything."

Barely able to catch his breath, aghast at Jo's treachery, Mattis reeled.

"But you're a locked door, no, an impenetrable fortress. Your secrets are your own and you are teaching me how closely you guard them. I must give a lot to get even a little, is that right?" Wanten asked. Mattis tried not to react and mostly succeeded.

Wanten turned on his heel and took two steps out of the cell. He spoke to the stormtrooper at the door. "If the boy tells us his name, right now, see to it that he's taken to a shared cell and given a clean blanket and mattress. But only if, right now, he tells us his name." Mattis didn't care about the blanket and the mattress—he'd grown up in a Durkteel orphanage—but he hoped with all the Force he could muster that they might put him in a cell with Lorica. And Lorica would know what to do. She always knew what to do.

Mattis told them his name.

CHAPTER

02

WANTEN LEFT THE CELL, pleased. It had taken him too long, but he had at least found the road to breaking the boy. Mattis Banz. The name meant nothing to Wanten, who in any case paid little attention to the details in the briefings he received from the First Order. He was, after all, merely a glorified caretaker for a crude detention facility on a fetid planet in the middle of nowhere.

Wanten's contemporaries, what few remained of them, were now officers in the First Order. But not Wanten. No, Wanten, for the greater part of his lifetime, skated from do-nothing position to do-less-than-nothing position, never given any real responsibility. He'd made one mistake, early in his career, when he was a stormtrooper for the Empire. He hadn't even been free of his teenaged years when it happened! And still, all this time later, he was being punished for it. They told him he was irresponsible. That he had no ambition. That he didn't try.

They were wrong. In those days, in his youth, he'd really tried hard. But the galaxy conspired against him, over and over. His eyesight was poor, so he was placed in an inferior squadron of shiftless stormtroopers. His helmet never fit correctly, and due to his Corellian nose, it was difficult to wear. His better eye was obstructed by the lenses, making him clumsy in the armor.

They sent him to Tatooine. It was hot. Wanten hated the heat. He hated breathing in his own smells in that sweaty helmet. And there was sand. So much sand. His armor wasn't vacuum-sealed or anything, and even now Wanten could easily conjure the grinding of grit and silt in its joints. It was a constant distraction. So could he really be blamed for not being quite as attentive as perhaps he ought to have been? Nothing interesting ever happened on Tatooine anyway.

Still, he'd been punished for things that

weren't really his fault. He'd been left to make sand castles on Tatooine while he watched as his friends and peers were promoted. He missed all the good battles—Endor, Jakku. Granted, he'd probably have been killed had he been there, but that kind of action was, Wanten often thought, preferable to running border checks on a planet no one cared to visit.

His time on that desert planet had given Wanten a lifetime antipathy for Hutts. Tatooine's crime lord ran the smuggling of weapons and spices, levied a water tax during drought, and coordinated the buying and selling of slaves, among other illegitimate businesses. There was an uneasy alliance between Jabba the Hutt's coterie and the occupying Empire forces. The Hutt was really in control of Tatooine. The Empire maintained a presence there only as a show of power. Or maybe they were on a mission? It had been such a long time ago on a planet so far away that Wanten couldn't remember.

One of the rare tiny pleasures Wanten took from his assignment on Vodran—a duty he'd been given, he knew, because there were no expectations of success, as well as little to bungle—was that it had, upon his arrival, been a Hutt stronghold.

Harra the Hutt, another disgusting personage like all of her kind, had built a palace upon the driest land she could find (which was still too swampy), consolidated the holdings of her predecessor by banishing or enslaving the natives of Vodran, and amassed a menagerie from all corners of the galaxy. It had made Wanten smile to order his troops to kill or expel everyone at Harra the Hutt's palace and to claim the throne room as his quarters. He still liked to look out of the high window to see the odd animal from her collection attempt to return "home." But there was no home for those creatures. They'd been set loose to live or die in the Vodran swamps, as there was no place there for Hutts any longer. Harra had escaped with her life. The First Order called it a failure of Wanten's leadership, but Wanten cared little. The Hutt was gone, and the palace was his. What hadn't fled or been killed—mostly service droids—was shuttled to a nearby moon with anything else Wanten or the First Order found useless.

After that, the drudgery began. Construction was not interesting to Wanten. It was mostly math. Wanten was bored by math. The First Order had contractors who made those plans. Wanten's responsibilities, which weren't many, were mainly to keep the younger recruits on task, to keep the perimeter fence erect so that animals didn't overtake the place, and to send weekly reports to the First Order. Those reports became so tedious, however, that Wanten's superiors at first began rescheduling their holo-calls and then canceled them altogether. All of which suited Wanten. He was prepared to live out the remainder of his days—which he suspected would also not be many—moist, warm, annoyed, and bored on this squishy planet. And then arrived Mattis Banz and his friends.

It was as if Monagha Schnelle, the fabled gift-giving red she-wolf from the holiday stories Wanten had heard as a youth, had arrived upon Vodran. These were children, yes, but they were also members of the Resistance and therefore might be valuable to Wanten's superiors. He must be careful not to present his prize to the First Order too soon, or they might claim it from under his nose and deny Wanten the credit he deserved. No, Wanten would press the children for information. He would squeeze them until their vital juices yielded something he could offer to his superiors, and then he would withhold even that! Yes, this was a wonderful plan. He'd make his own bosses bring him to the supreme leaders themselves! They would certainly promote him to a righteous place in the First Order then.

Wanten was still smiling as he made his way through the barracks, across the sodden Fold, and into the main throne room, where the Jerjerrod boy awaited him. The boy stiffened when Wanten entered. Of course the boy would be nervous. His arrival at Wanten's compound was degrading. The Jerjerrods were among the First Order's elite. That their progeny would be so coarsely escorted by lowly stormtroopers was an embarrassment. This boy couldn't know that Wanten respected those old Empire families, those dynasties that had not wavered in their devotion to a better galaxy through any means necessary, from the monarchy that rose from the Old Republic to this new First Order. It would be Wanten's job to put the boy at ease. Then Jo Jerjerrod would tell Wanten all he needed to know.

"Is Mattis okay?" Jo asked, once Wanten was seated on what used to be Harra the Hutt's throne. Wanten had ordered the stormtroopers who arrived with him months before to make alterations so that a non-Hutt might be comfortable upon it. They hadn't done an outstanding job; these First Order stormtroopers didn't hold a candle to the troops in Wanten's day, as far as he was concerned, but the addition of some cushions and blocks of wood to approximate something more chair-like was sufficient.

"Is it possible that this boy is your friend?" Wanten asked. The way he said *friend* made it sound like profanity. "What would your parents say? I'm pretty sure they don't have friends. People in the Empire"—Wanten corrected himself—"in the First Order don't have *friends*."

"He was in my squadron, sir."

Wanten nodded. Whether or not Mattis was Jo's friend made little difference to him. Both Jo and those with whom he'd arrived were a means to an end. Wanten scanned the room and took in the two stormtroopers who flanked him wherever he went. He assumed they weren't interested in his conversation with his captive.

"He wasn't helpful to me, if you were wondering," Wanten said playfully.

"He wouldn't be," Jo replied. "He's too well trained to tell you anything right away."

Wanten nodded for Jo to continue.

"Mattis, Lorica, and Aygee-Ninety may be new recruits, but the Resistance isn't so ineffectual that they wouldn't train their people for this contingency. They'll keep quiet for a while, sir. They'll try to figure out a way to escape or to contact the Resistance for rescue."

"Luckily," Wanten said, "I have you."

Jo shook his head and looked disappointed. "I can't help you," he said.

"What can you possibly mean?"

"Mattis and the others? They know more than I do."

"You were in their squadron, weren't you? You say you were." Wanten narrowed his eyes.

"I was," Jo said. "But they didn't trust me. None of them did, not even the Resistance commanders. So, I know some things—rules of conduct, a few names—but they know more."

"And they won't tell me anything today," Wanten confirmed.

Jo nodded. "Nor tomorrow, sir."

"Do you recommend a course of action, Mr. Jerjerrod, to circumvent the Resistance's training?" Wanten asked. He really was curious. Jo came from an Imperial dynasty. Would he possess the same cunning, strategic mind as his parents and grandparents?

Jo said, "Put them in a cell together. All three

of them. They're not good soldiers; though they know some of the protocols, they're undisciplined. They'll talk amongst themselves, as long as they're relatively unguarded."

"Are you suggesting I leave my prisoners unregulated?"

"No, sir. Just . . . have your guards maintain some distance. Allow Mattis and Lorica and Aygee to feel comfortable enough to talk. Maybe . . . How big are your cells? I mean, how many can they hold?"

"Some hold four prisoners."

"You could place a fourth in with them. Someone they'll feel relaxed enough to be candid in front of but who will, out of self-preservation, report back to you."

Wanten nodded. It was a good plan. But Wanten wasn't stupid, and he didn't completely trust this boy.

"I will place them in a cell together," Wanten told Jo. The boy seemed pleased. That wouldn't last another moment, if Wanten had his way. These people had to be reminded who their commander was. "Just the two," Wanten added. "Eliminate the droid."

"Eliminate?" The boy sounded shocked.

"Like the rest of the service droids and dregs that Harra the Hutt left behind, this machine, which was for some reason allowed into the Resistance, will be jettisoned from this mud planet," Wanten said in a voice that dared Jo to question him.

Jo did. "With all due respect, sir," he said, "Aygee-Ninety was allowed in the Resistance as a recruit, not just a service droid. It's possible there was a reason for that."

Wanten rolled his eyes. "It's possible," he said. "But I don't care. I don't care for droids, especially droids who act above their station. Your droid seems that type."

"He isn't *my* droid, sir," Jo sniffed. "In fact, his owner is far from here, having fled the planet without a look back. His owner was a quality mechanic."

"What are you saying, Mr. Jerjerrod?" Wanten was impatient with the boy.

"There might be value in the droid, sir. I don't mean to be impertinent or question your decision."

"And yet, you've done both."

Jo tried again. "Let it be my pet project," he said. "Allow me to reprogram Aygee-Ninety.

Perhaps I can make a First Order soldier of him. If I can devise a quick and efficient way to do that, wouldn't the First Order want to reward my commander for allowing me the opportunity?"

Wanten laughed without smiling. "You're not as cunning as you think you are, young man. You've spent some time with this droid and wish to continue to do so. But, yes, your notion intrigues me. Reprogram the droid. Make him one of ours. Maybe he'll be the spy in that cell!"

"Programming the levels required for deception is beyond me, I'm afraid. Mattis and Lorica would know right away."

Wanten deflated. "I suppose if I can't be tricky, I can at least be cruel. It would be funny to make the reprogrammed droid their guard, wouldn't it?"

"Yes, sir. It would."

"Good, then! I've made a wonderful plan." Wanten clapped his hands together. The smacking sound was loud in the echoing throne room, empty but for the few stormtroopers, Jo, and Wanten. "You there." Wanten motioned to one of the stormtroopers. "Take Mr. Jerjerrod and collect that droid, then take them both to the Garage."

"Yes, sir," the stormtrooper agreed, and started out.

Before Jo could exit the room, however, Wanten stopped him. "Mr. Jerjerrod," he said. Jo turned back. "You'll have supper with me tonight, I hope? It'd be a treat to hear some of those insignificant details about the Resistance with which you are acquainted."

Jo nodded dutifully. "Yes, sir. It'd be my pleasure."

"Very good," Wanten said. "Your hard work spying for the First Order will finally come to fruition, boy. And we'll both be thanked for it."

Jo turned on his heel and left. Wanten looked around the throne room. Unable to find anything else with which to occupy his time, the detention center commander clasped his fleshy hands together and stared into the middle distance.

CHAPTER

03

THE STORMTROOPERS deposited Lorica in a double-wide chamber, dank and slick with a dirty film. There were two bunk beds along either wall and on each bunk a thin, filthy mattress. Lorica dropped onto one of the bottom bunks. She was exhausted. She was angry. She didn't know whom to blame for this embarrassing capture by the First Order, but it wasn't her fault.

She'd been a good soldier for the Resistance. She felt joining the Resistance was her duty, especially after all the rumors about her heroism on her home planet. They were rumors that weren't true, but that Lorica hadn't corrected. She wasn't a hero before, but she would work hard to become one in the Resistance. She followed the rules. She made herself indispensible to Jo, her squad leader. Yet she'd still wound up on Vodran, sent there by Admiral Ackbar as punishment for a fiasco in which she'd really played no role. Then that, too, had gone awry, and here she was in a First Order detention center that was as busted and scruffy as the squadron of which she'd been part.

Yes, Lorica was angry. She wished there was something to kick in this grimy cell. She was afraid that if she kicked the bed, the whole thing would collapse, and she didn't see a kindhearted stormtrooper coming in to repair it for her. She had to do violence to something, though, so she leaped from the bed and took the mattress with her. She hurled it against the cell's back wall. It wasn't satisfying, soft as the mattress was, and following it with a hurricane of rough blankets didn't cause the destruction she was after. She decided to kick the bunk bed after all. She kicked it a bunch of times, then she kicked it a bunch more. It hurt her feet, but the hurt felt good, felt like action, and she kept kicking and kicking and kicking until kicking wasn't enough. She grabbed the frame and yanked it down to the floor. The metal screeched and wrenched and, as she'd predicted, fell apart.

Not through yet, Lorica grasped the bunk bed opposite her and gave that a yank. It was heavier than the first one, but not by much, and she sent that one crashing to the floor, too.

"Aaaaaaaaar!"

Lorica thought she'd gone so far into her rageful haze that the scream had come from her own mouth. It took her a moment to realize that the screaming—as well as some thrashing—came from the mess of blankets that had tumbled onto the floor. Lorica stumbled back a few steps and watched as the thrashing subsided. A stick-thin woman who might have been ten or a hundred years older than Lorica yanked the coverings from over her head. She continued to sit in the nest of blankets, her enormous eyes never resting on one object, her large head framed by an avalanche of frizzled dark hair.

"What are you?" the woman spat.

"You mean, *who* am I?" Lorica countered. After her initial surprise, Lorica had quickly switched to a defensive position. Her body was braced for a fight; her hands were balled into fists.

"You're pink!" the woman on the floor squealed, then chittered out what must have been laughter.

"I'm not *pink*." Lorica bristled.

The woman sprang from her squatting position and placed herself centimeters from Lorica's face. Lorica flinched, but the woman matched her movement swiftly, like a synchronized dance.

"You're pinker than me, and me is the only one I know!" The woman snapped a couple of times in Lorica's face, and Lorica swatted her hand away. The woman chirped out another laugh and fell back onto the pile of blankets.

"Are you insane?" Lorica asked. It was the kind of flippant question she often threw at her friends (and enemies). Asking this woman, she was genuinely curious. The woman looked up at Lorica, then away, at Lorica, then away again.

Lorica decided to try a gentler tactic. She forced her fists to unclench and her teeth to ungrit. She relaxed the muscles in her face. "What's your name?" she asked in a slightly less mean voice. Sounding slightly less mean was as nice as Lorica tended to be.

The woman studied the ceiling, as if she'd once written her name there in case someone asked. She studied for a while, as if the name she'd written up there was very long and complicated. When she looked again to Lorica, it was with an expression of deep consideration.

Something easier, then, Lorica told herself. "My name is Lorica Demaris. My friends and I were brought here by stormtroopers."

The woman pulled back her lips in a scowl. She had rows and rows of tiny sharp teeth. "Those shuck-jackets. They're mean ones, yeh?"

Lorica nodded. So the woman didn't like the stormtroopers. They had that in common, at least. "They're bad," Lorica agreed. She righted the unbroken bunk she'd pushed over and pulled the mattress back onto it, then sat on it cross-legged.

"So bad. When I tell them about the scootling in the walls, they bang on the bars there and they count me out."

It wasn't surprising that the stormtroopers were foul to the woman. She was annoying and panicky and hard to understand. "Scootling in the walls?" What could that mean? It was too difficult a question, Lorica thought, if the woman couldn't even come up with her own name.

The woman popped up, wrapped the blankets around her, and bounded onto the bunk beside Lorica. She was appreciably calmer. "Cost Niktur," she said.

"Are you putting a curse on me?" Lorica asked. It wasn't out of the realm of possibility that the woman was some sort of scary witch. Though she *was* less scary with every moment.

"Cost Niktur!" the woman said again, gleefully.

"Ahh, that's your name," Lorica replied. "Right? Cost?"

"Cost, yes, me and I. We're Cost." The woman, Cost Niktur, smiled with all of her jagged teeth and nodded a few times. Abruptly, though, she stopped and jerked her head in the direction of the cell's back wall. "You hear?" she demanded. "You hear? The scootling! They won't come— they'll bang the bars and tell me the scootling is *inside*. But it isn't inside. It's inside out!" She leaped from the bed and ran around the cell, throwing blankets around in a frenzy, as Lorica had done in anger.

"Hey, hey . . ." Lorica stood and made what she hoped were calming motions. They caught Cost's attention but only for a few seconds. Between breaths, Cost flapped around the cell, pounding on the back wall and hissing. "You have to calm down," Lorica began again. She didn't think it would do much good to reason with Cost, and she didn't get a chance anyway because just then the stormtroopers arrived.

"You there. Shut up," the stormtrooper in front commanded. He banged a couple of times on the bars of their cell. "Get her to shut up," he snapped at Lorica.

"I'm trying!" she snapped right back. The stormtrooper smacked his club against the cell door. Lorica shook her head. It wouldn't pay to make enemies of her guards, but neither was she one to back down.

The stormtrooper stalked up to the bars and laid his fists against them. "You, Resistance blossom, don't you test me. Tell your friend to shut up and you shut up, too!"

Lorica couldn't take it. All the anger and frustration of the past few days—the past few months—frothed up in her chest until she couldn't contain it. She stormed the few steps to the bars where the stormtrooper sneered at her. He wore a helmet, but Lorica could tell he was sneering. She grabbed the bars closest to the stormtrooper's black lenses and shook as hard as she could. The cage rattled, the stormtrooper jumped back, and Cost stopped yelling just as Lorica, having nothing left to say, roared a throaty howl at her captor. She let go of the bars, but they continued to shake—*ping-ping-ping*—against the concrete until they were silent, too.

"Open the cell door," the stormtrooper said coldly, batting his blunt weapon in his open palm.

"Don't open that door!" The voice came from somewhere out of Lorica's line of vision.

The stormtrooper hesitated a moment, then stood down. "Yes, sir," he said.

The person who'd spoken strode into view. He was younger than Lorica had expected for someone with such a commanding voice. He couldn't have been much older than Lorica herself. He had jet-black hair that was too fine to be cut in the short military style favored by the First Order, so it swept across his forehead and fell into his dark eyes. He wore a stiff, stern look that softened when he met Lorica's gaze through the bars.

In the back of the cell, Cost paced, muttering to herself. Lorica picked out words like *noise* and *scootling*.

"Aren't you worried your cape will get muddy out here?" Lorica asked the new arrival. She tried to sound as defiant as possible.

"I have several," answered the guard, if that's

what he was. "And you'd be surprised what good housekeepers these stormtroopers are. Right, Ceezee-Ten-Seven-Six?"

"Sir, I feel as if you're telling me that I'll be on housekeeping duty," the angry stormtrooper replied. Lorica stifled a laugh. She didn't like this new arrival—he was the enemy after all—but she did like his sense of humor.

"That's precisely what you'll be doing, Ceezee-Ten-Seven-Six. You're dismissed."

"This little *blossom*—"

"That will be all."

The stormtrooper huffed inside his helmet, then lied, "Static, sir. Sorry." He marched away down the corridor.

Before his footfalls had even disappeared, his commander turned with purpose to Lorica. "Don't taunt your guards," he said. Any good humor he'd had was gone now. "Or I'll be forced to keep a closer eye on your cell myself."

"You seem more reasonable than these nerf wranglers," Lorica said.

"I'm not. I promise."

"What's your name, boss?" Lorica tried to keep her voice casual and fearless, but she couldn't deny the discomfort rising inside her. It wasn't anger, as before. It was something else. Something unfamiliar. Something almost like fear.

"Ingo Salik. And please don't forget that I *am* the boss. These stormtroopers work for me. I report directly to Commander Wanten."

"Sounds important."

"You're trying to be diminishing, but it won't work. My role here *is* important. Things don't have to be adversarial—"

"I'm in a cage," Lorica pointed out.

"Things needn't be difficult, then. We can get along, if we each know our respective places. You, me, her." He pointed to Cost. "Them." He jerked his thumb at the stormtroopers. "We all behave, and things are easy."

"Then behave," Lorica said, swallowing the catalogue of insults she wanted to shout at Ingo.

He broke into that soft smile again. "I know *I* will. As a show of goodwill, how about I give you a friend?"

"Besides her, you mean?" Lorica tipped her head back toward Cost.

Ingo turned to the stormtroopers and said, "Fetch the other one. Wanten is done with him. Put him in here, so they can plan their escape together."

As the stormtroopers marched away, Lorica screwed up her face at Ingo.

"What?" he asked innocently. "You'd be stupid not to talk about it, at least! I know you're too smart to just sit here and accept your fate."

"I guess I'll see you on the other side of these bars then," Lorica agreed.

"Oh, you won't succeed," Ingo assured her. "I'm good at this. We may be a new facility, but we haven't had any escapees. A few eaten by a rancor out in the Fold, but we've maintained the perimeter fence better since then."

"Too bad. Inside of a rancor would've been a great way out of here."

Ingo laughed quietly. He possessed a calmness that Lorica was sure kept his prisoners tranquil as well. Before he could offer another agreeable parry, the stormtroopers returned, escorting Mattis. They stopped when they got to Lorica's cell.

"I'm going to have them open the cell door to let your friend in," Ingo told her. "You won't run, will you?"

Lorica smiled. "Of course not. Like you said: I'm too smart."

Ingo motioned to a control box on the wall

by the cell, and a stormtrooper stepped to it and punched in some numbers. The bars slid open, and as soon as the opening was wide enough, Lorica burst out. She knocked over the trooper who'd opened the cell and was halfway down the hall when she heard Ingo sigh, "Stop her, please."

She heard the pop of the blaster before she crackled with a sharp blue energy that she could feel in her teeth, then in her bones, all in a matter of seconds. She was unconscious before she hit the ground.

Lorica awoke back in her cell. The mattresses had been replaced and the blankets reset. Cost was back in her bunk, rocking and watching the rear wall anxiously. Lorica was in the bunk opposite her. A pair of feet dangled in her face.

"Good morning," Mattis said, hopping off the bunk above her.

Lorica looked to the windowless back wall, where Cost paced back and forth, inspecting its corners. "How do you know?" she asked.

"That it's morning? Well, I went to sleep, then I woke up," Mattis replied.

"That tracks. Kind of . . ." Lorica tried to stand, but her legs wouldn't support her. Mattis caught her by the arm and lowered her back onto the bunk. She didn't lie down. She needed to remain alert. She glared at Mattis. "You know your sleep schedule doesn't dictate *actual* day and night," she said.

Mattis shot her a goofy grin, the only kind he had. "Aw, you're just mad because you got stun-blasted."

Lorica went to retort, but all that came out of her mouth was sour vomit. It poured out thin and watery, thanks to the little food she'd eaten in the past two days, collecting in a puddle at her feet.

Mattis laughed. "Is that all you have to say for yourself?" he said.

"What are you so chipper about?" Lorica asked, wiping her mouth.

"Oh, I've accepted our doom," Mattis said. He backed onto Cost's bunk and sat down on it. "We're prisoners of the First Order, Jo was a traitor all along, this crazy person is talking to the walls. . . ."

Cost paused and cocked her head, birdlike, at Mattis and said, "I'm hollering at the scooter in the walls, ya shrubb!" She knelt down where the wall met the floor and muttered something.

Then, as an afterthought to Mattis, she added, "Walls don't talk anyways."

"What do you mean Jo was a traitor all along?" Lorica demanded. Fueled by this revelation, she got to her feet, where she stayed only briefly. She wobbled and Mattis helped her sit down, which she liked less than being dizzy in the first place.

"Tell me what happened."

Mattis told her about Wanten and how the facility's commander didn't seem to care what Mattis told him because Jo was spilling everything he knew about the Resistance. "He was pretending the whole time," Mattis said. "We shouldn't have trusted him."

"He explained himself to us!" Lorica yelled, startling Cost, who bellowed incoherently as her pacing around the cell grew furious.

"He told us his parents are in the First Order," Mattis said. Lorica shook her head. She couldn't hear him clearly over Cost's wailing. "The First Order," Mattis said louder. "His parents are in it. That's what he told us!"

"That doesn't mean *he* is! Besides, he saved our lives!"

"We saved his!" Mattis yelled. It wasn't a good

argument, but for some reason he felt it needed saying. "Besides—" He was too loud now, as Cost had quieted and was busying herself in the corner of the cell. "Sorry. Besides, wouldn't saving us be the best thing for a traitor to do? Then we'd really think he was on our side. Which we did."

"We did because he was. He *is*." Lorica was certain of Jo's loyalty. She had to be. She'd served him in the squadron, and she wouldn't serve a traitor. "People aren't just what other people say they are."

"He tried to wipe Aygee's memory," Mattis reminded her.

"I was there. He wasn't going to do it. Probably."

Mattis shrugged. "I don't want it to be true, either," he said. "But even if he wasn't spying, even if he isn't a traitor, he is now. He's not in here with us, is he?" Mattis motioned around the cell. Cost started wailing again and kicking at the walls.

"Can you stop that?" Lorica snapped, but Cost didn't notice.

"He's saving himself by selling us out," Mattis said, disappointed. He rubbed his head and stared at the ground.

"You don't know that's true."

"But for our own sakes, shouldn't we assume it is? Aygee is gone, probably scrapped or worse. Wanten told me that Jo is talking. I don't want it to be true, not after we lost Dec and Sari, and after what happened to Klimo . . . but . . ." Mattis lifted his head to see her face.

Lorica looked at Mattis through angry half-closed eyes. She shook her head slowly, only just understanding how much she had liked Klimo. She realized their last hope was Dec, the least reliable person she had ever known, and his friend Sari, who had never liked her.

"Lorica, we only have each other here," Mattis said. "No one is coming for us."

CHAPTER

04

*P*ING . . . *PING* . . .

Where was that other shuttle? The plan had been that when they were finished on Vodran, they were to signal the cargo ship that had brought them to the Si'Klaata Cluster to meet their shuttles and return J-Squadron to the Resistance base. But now Dec couldn't raise the cargo ship. And worse, he couldn't find the second shuttle.

During the terror of the rancor attack, Dec and Sari had managed to fly one shuttle to safety. As they were leaving, they saw Klimo commandeer the second shuttle. Klimo wasn't the best pilot among them—Dec wagered that was his brother,

AG-90—but the rest of them, AG, Mattis, Jo, and Lorica, were near enough that Klimo could pick them up quickly and one of them could maneuver the shuttle into the atmosphere and away from the rancor pack. Only—that should have happened immediately. They were, Dec had thought, right behind him.

He'd already talked Sari out of returning to the planet's surface to make sure the others weren't still there. He didn't want to risk landing in the midst of another rancor scrap, and anyway, he trusted his own eyes. Klimo was in the shuttle. The others were nearby. There was no way they'd have missed the chance to escape.

So where was that other shuttle?

Ping . . . ping . . .

In J-Squadron, Jo had taught them to use a ping scanner on the comms to probe nearby space for objects. Sari, who had been anxious ever since the other shuttle hadn't shown up behind them right away, hadn't left the communications bank in what had to be a full day. She just sat there, still caked in the dried muck of Vodran, sending tiny signals into outer space. Thus far, the only contact made was with some large hunks of debris. Vodran didn't even have a moon where Dec might land their shuttle to rest and recuperate. They just spun around and around the small planet, hoping for word from their friends.

They weren't talking much to each other, either, not after the initial panic had subsided. Sari was mad at Dec for refusing to return to Vodran. She was tired and worried and itchy from the mud. He was, too. It was easier not to talk.

Ping . . . ping . . .

An echoing beacon sent out to nowhere. As he listened to each signal, Dec grew sadder. His brother was out there somewhere. His friends, too. After all they'd been through together, Dec thought of them all as friends. Even Jo, with whom he'd sparred so relentlessly. He hoped they were all right. He needed them to be all right.

Ping . . . ping . . .

"Dec."

He was so lulled by the gentle pinging from the adjacent bay, and so lost in reflection, that Dec didn't register Sari's voice until she spoke again more forcefully.

"Dec!"

"You got something?" Dec asked, swinging

around in the pilot's chair to face the communications bay. The shuttle could fly itself for a few minutes.

"Yeah, but I don't know what."

Dec made his way to the comms bay to join her. Sari was hunched in the small space as she had been for the past day. She was a large girl, thick-trunked, and muscular. She looked, thanks to the sludge, like a small hill. Her hair fell in a heavy dirty-blond lock over her bulbous forehead.

"Listen," she said, and twiddled some dials on the communicators.

Ping . . . ping . . .

Dec was hopeful for a few seconds, but that feeling quickly faded when Sari's fiddling produced nothing but the silence and rhythmic pinging to which they'd been listening for the past several hours. He shook his head but stopped before she could look up to see him do it. He chalked up her excitement to her optimism, her hope. But that was all it was. Hope. Nothing real.

Until.

Ping . . . p—

She moved another dial and the pinging stopped. Static stuttered over the communicator.

"What's—" Dec started to say, but Sari shushed him, holding up a finger for him to wait.

She returned to the board and again moved dials and pressed buttons.

"Read us . . . unknown . . . please . . ." The words came over the communicator choppy and indistinct. It was a man's voice, that much was evident, but all the technology it passed through rendered it robotic and unfamiliar. It could be Jo or Mattis, for sure. It might even be AG.

Dec grabbed the communicator. "Aygee? Is that you, Brother?"

Sari grabbed it back from him. "Wait!" she said. "What if it isn't—"

The comms squealed with static, and Sari dropped the communicator.

"It's them, it's gotta be," Dec said. His voice came out more desperate-sounding than he wanted. He hadn't realized until that moment how deeply worried he was about his brother.

The voice returned. *"Identify yourself . . ."* It came in more clearly now. It wasn't AG. It wasn't Jo or Mattis or Lorica, either. *"Unknown shuttle, identify yourself."*

Dec and Sari locked eyes. What should they

do? Dec put a finger to his lips. Stay quiet for now.

"Unknown shuttle, you are encroaching on private airspace. Please identify yourself."

Dec grabbed Sari's shoulder. He hadn't meant to, but he was scared. He needed something solid to hold on to. She patted his hand.

"Unknown vessel, we will give you one chance to reply. After that, you will be considered hostile and sentry shuttles will be deployed to intercept."

Dec swallowed hard. They had to do something. He grabbed the communicator. "Uh . . ." he said. Not a great start. "We are . . . we're real lost, man," he said. Sari looked at him and slapped her forehead. "We musta taken a wrong turn around Corson Prime, got turned around. . . ." He wasn't sure what else to say, but the voice on the other end of the comm was quiet, so maybe Dec's ruse had worked?

"Deploying three sentry shuttles," the voice came back. *"Remain where you are."*

Dec and Sari immediately leaped to their feet. Sari hit her head on the bay's ceiling, then slammed a hand on the communications bank, shutting it down.

"Let's definitely not remain where we are," she said.

"Definitely not," Dec agreed. He scrambled to the pilot's chair. "We gotta get out of here," he said.

"Fast, please," Sari said.

Already, through the viewport, they saw three tiny shuttles taking off from Vodran and climbing into the atmosphere. They grew larger quickly. They were First Order sentries, and they were coming fast!

"First Order?" Dec cried out.

"First Order! Punch it!" Sari yelled.

Dec punched it. Their shuttle juddered then spun off into space. He didn't know where they would go; he just knew they needed to fly away from there.

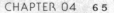

CHAPTER
05

MATTIS DIDN'T REMEMBER FALLING asleep. He was sitting on the bunk opposite Lorica, both of them trying not to look at each other. She wasn't giving in, wouldn't allow for the truth that Jo had betrayed them. She slouched on her bunk taking shallow breaths, her eyelids half-shuttered, her skin a darker shade of pink than usual. For his part, Mattis couldn't argue anymore, either. He wanted to win the argument; he needed her to understand that he was right. He also needed her on his side for what was to come. Simultaneously, he just didn't want her angry at him; he wanted Lorica to think warmly of him, for reasons he wasn't quite ready to explore or understand. He fidgeted on his bunk, both wanting and not wanting to convince her further, until finally he succumbed, at some point, to sleep.

He knew they'd slept because they were woken roughly by their guards. It was the same haughty lead trooper from the day before. Even if he hadn't had the scarred lens on his helmet, Mattis would have known this trooper by the glee with which he roused the prisoners. He clanged his baton across the bars, back and forth, back and forth, shouting for them to get on their feet. Mattis had started thinking of this stormtrooper as "Patch," and he feared him more than the others.

Mattis jumped up from Cost's bed, where he'd fallen asleep, smacking his head on the upper bunk. He cried out in pain. He was sure the breathy line of static he heard was the stormtrooper laughing. Patch told them to stand at attention by their bunks.

Lorica pretended a casual stance, leaning back on her bunk as if she'd woken by choice. She kept her gaze on the ceiling, not acknowledging either the stormtrooper or her cellmates. Mattis did his best to look obedient, but he was sending Lorica signals with his mind: *Look at me, look at me, look at me.* She didn't, which made him angry at his nascent Jedi powers. When would they fully develop? Didn't the Force know he needed it right now?

Cost emerged from the shadowy corner of the cell like a phantom. Had she been down on the concrete floor all night? If she had, she didn't seem to mind. Taking a place opposite Mattis, she smiled, showing him all her rows of teeth.

"You all good friends now?" the stormtrooper asked.

"The best," Lorica said dryly. "We picked out each other's outfits and did each other's hair all night."

"Good," the trooper said, not caring about Lorica's sarcasm and punching a code into the pad by their cell door. "You're gonna need friends in the Fold."

He herded them out of the cell in a tight group and led them through the corridor and outside. Mattis tried again to get Lorica's attention, brushing her hand lightly as they walked. She shook her head, resolute. She didn't want to talk, he figured. She didn't want to plan.

The Fold was a small muddy space between the walls of the palace and the detention cells. Wire fences enclosed either side. Some round stone tables were clustered at one end; slabs of rock meant for sitting upon surrounded each table. An ongeball screen was affixed to the far wall, and a few dodgy-looking prisoners played aggressively beneath it. They seemed more interested in the rough jostling the game allowed than in making plays to toss the ongeball into the screen.

The stormtrooper who'd led them outside stopped a few steps from the door.

"Welcome to the Fold," he said. "You'll get mud on your boots. There are no other boots. So clean your boots before you return to your cell. There's a lather brush hanging there. Don't take it off of there. If you take it off of there, you'll be punished."

Patch motioned to the opposite end of the Fold. "Those are tables. You may sit at them. They're planted in the ground, so you can't throw them."

Mattis didn't think he could throw a stone table that size, but he appreciated that they probably weren't so worried about someone like him as they were about prisoners like the tough blue Squamatan woman or the brutish Gigoran from whom she was trying to steal the ongeball.

"Go ahead and make more friends," the stormtrooper said, turning on his heel and leaving them. The door to the block slammed closed behind him with a metallic echo.

Cost slipped her slender hand into Mattis's. He shook it loose. Cost looked dejected, though that expression faded quickly as she became distracted by the ongeball game being played. There was nothing playful about it. Prisoners of the First Order, cooped up in their cells for most of their hours, took full advantage of both their time outside and their propensity for violence. Hands, pads, paws, and claws snatched and punched at torsos covered in a leathery hide or thick pelt or solid muscle. Mattis didn't know what the teams were—there were usually three in ongeball—and it didn't appear to matter to the players. They seemed to just throw themselves at one another haphazardly, like meteors crashing.

"Fun and games!" Cost yipped, clapping her palms together. She started for the fray, but Mattis pulled her back.

"Stay with us for a little while," he said, looking over Cost's head at Lorica, who watched the ongeball match intently. "Let's go sit on those . . . slabs," he said, guiding Cost toward the tables where sat a depressed Ortolan, a Yarkora with some sort of gloppy crust that had worn away his skin, and a tiny, still Kailynn whose Dathomirian tattoos did little to hide her sadness.

"Don't talk to anyone," Lorica told Mattis.

"Don't talk to anyone," Mattis told Cost. Cost smiled and continued her slow, uneven walk, weaving precariously close to the ongeball match. "Cost," Mattis hissed, trying not to draw any attention to himself. "Watch out you don't—" But he didn't finish his thought because, even as he reached out to nudge Cost away from the combatants, a sweaty, moss-hued Gamorrean blundered out of the match and crashed into Mattis.

Mattis opened his eyes to find the Gamorrean fully in his face; the creature's tusks were chipped and yellow. He snorted angrily at Mattis, a series of grunts and snorfs relaying his upset.

"I'm sorry," Mattis whined. He didn't mean to whine, but he was scared and the wind was knocked out of him. He put his arms up, trying to look innocent and apologetic, hoping the Gamorrean—most of whom spoke Galactic Basic—understood. Whether or not he did, however, was moot, as the porcine bruiser answered

Mattis with a hard shove, sending him back into the mud.

The Gamorrean pulled himself up to his full not-very-impressive height as he was flanked by the beastly Gigoran and a compact snaggletoothed Snivvian.

"He doesn't like you," the Snivvian told Mattis.

"That's okay," Mattis said, trying to be agreeable. He looked around for Lorica and Cost, who'd made their way to the tables already.

The white-furred Gigoran growled and dipped her head.

"I'm sorry," Mattis said to her. "I'm not worth the effort."

This self-deprecating defense made the Snivvian laugh, a sort of moaning wheeze. He clapped the Gamorrean on the back and both of them returned to the ongeball match, grunting and laughing. But the Gigoran didn't go with them. She took a stride closer to Mattis and patted down some of her fur. It was barely white anymore, caked with mud and filth as it was. She growled again. Mattis didn't know what she was saying. What Mattis did know was that, like her friends, she didn't like him.

The Gigoran grumbled.

"Her name is Ymmoss," said Cost, suddenly standing just outside of the Gigoran's radius.

"Thanks?" Mattis said, hoping that neither the Gigoran nor the other prisoners could hear his teeth clashing together in fear. "I'm M-Mattis," he said to the Gigoran.

The Gigoran, Ymmoss, roared, raising her thick arms aggressively.

"Ymmoss says she's gonna eat you for la-la-lunch!" Cost said in a singsong.

"What?" Mattis yelled, shuffling back across the ground. "Why? What did I do?" He scuttled back even more until he was up against the wall. "I don't even know her! She doesn't even know me! I'm really nice! I don't—"

He was cut off by Ymmoss's crazed growl and the sight of the Gigoran striding toward him, arms outstretched. "Mrrrooowr!" Ymmoss bellowed and lifted Mattis off his feet. Mattis had a brief flashback to his life on Durkteel, so many months before, when that bully Fikk had lifted him up and spun him around. But this wasn't like that. Fikk had been a teenaged Saurin and, while strong, he wasn't an angry full-grown Gigoran. A Gigoran whom, Mattis noted, was a prisoner in this detention center and therefore likely some sort of criminal. Ymmoss might tear Mattis's limbs off and enjoy them as an appetizer to the lunch she apparently intended to make of him.

She held Mattis aloft, one giant paw under his neck and the other propping up his legs. His view was only of sky, and he wished on the Force for a ship to appear and take him out of there. But none came. Instead, Ymmoss spun and hurled Mattis into the ongeball match, scattering the players. He landed atop the Gamorrean he'd angered earlier, and both of them tumbled into the muck. The Gamorrean snorted but scrambled away when he saw Ymmoss stalking toward them, roaring and thumping a fist into her large open palm.

Mattis didn't know what he'd done to deserve being smashed by a vicious Gigoran, but he clenched his eyes closed and waited for his death.

Instead, he heard a loud thump, followed by a cracking sound and another furious roar.

Mattis opened his eyes. He wasn't dead; the sound hadn't been his skull cracking between two enormous Gigoran paws. So what had made that noise?

Past his feet, on the ground some meters away,

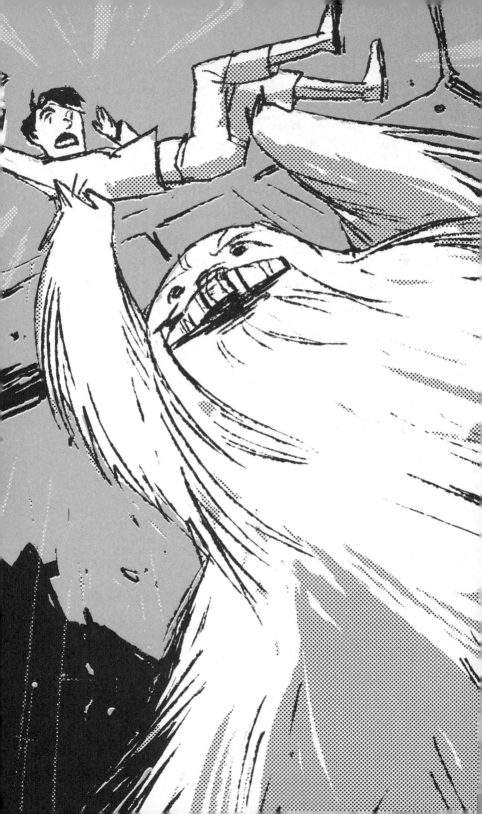

Lorica sat atop Ymmoss, holding the Gigoran down and stroking the side of her face. Ymmoss groaned a high-pitched whine, but allowed Lorica to continue. Mattis shook his head. He had to be hallucinating.

Propping himself on his elbows for a better look, he caught the Gigoran's eye and she gave a terrific roar, throwing Lorica off her and rising to go after Mattis again.

"Hey!" Lorica shouted, pulling herself up from her tumble. "I broke one finger. I don't have to stop there."

Ymmoss cocked her big head at Lorica and bared her teeth. She made a few explanatory growling noises.

"She says her problem isn't with you, even though you broke her finger," Cost told Lorica.

"I don't care," Lorica informed Cost, never taking her eyes from Ymmoss.

The Gigoran groaned.

"You should care," Cost said.

"I've been told that a lot," Lorica said, and launched herself again at Ymmoss. This time, though, the Gigoran was ready for her. She went to bat Lorica away, but Lorica was fast, so instead of a strong, resolute whack, the best Ymmoss managed was a half swat that, from a Gigoran, was still pretty powerful. It didn't send Lorica flying back from whence she came, as Ymmoss might have hoped, but it did put her on the ground.

Mattis panicked, of course. He'd have hoped he'd show more courage in a situation like this, but he'd never been in a situation like this. He'd never really thought of being in a situation like this. Attacked by an enraged Gigoran for no reason at all? Who would think of that? Not Mattis! No one Mattis could think of would think of it! Mattis had always thought his confrontations would be seen from an X-wing cockpit. Hand-to-hand combat was terrifying to him.

Though not to Lorica, obviously. Once on the ground, she swept with her leg, catching the Gigoran behind her knee. Ymmoss buckled but didn't fall. Lorica did, however, now have Ymmoss's full attention.

"He's with me," Lorica hissed. "You attack him, you attack me, and I'm not afraid of an overgrown lint ball."

"I am," Mattis chirped. Lorica silenced him with a look.

Off to the side, Cost cleared her throat loudly.

"What?" Lorica said.

Cost cleared her throat again.

Rolling her eyes, Lorica added, "She's with me, too, I guess. So, no hurting either of them."

Ymmoss roared.

"She's not afraid of you," Cost translated.

"Fine," Lorica retorted. "Like I said, the feeling's mutual."

Another cry came from Ymmoss, and the Gigoran wheeled around and lunged for Lorica. She managed to swat her this time, and Lorica hurled backward into the Snivvian and Gamorrean, who'd paused their game to watch the fracas. The Snivvian lifted Lorica up, and she shook him off abruptly.

"Don't help," she said.

"Don't worry," he replied, laughing.

By now, Ymmoss had turned back to Mattis. Mattis rallied all of his courage, took a deep breath, and charged the Gigoran. He didn't think he'd actually do her any harm, but maybe he would succeed in not embarrassing himself completely. As he ran, Ymmoss swung at him; through some dumb instinct, Mattis ducked and found himself in her very close personal radius. He could smell the thick odor of her fur. Both Ymmoss and Mattis were surprised to find Mattis in such close proximity, and both paused before Mattis regained his sense and punched the Gigoran as hard as he could in her chest.

Nothing.

It was as if an insect had bumped into her midflight, only less annoying. Ymmoss looked down at him from her great height and bellowed an enormous spittle-filled roar, her hot, meaty breath clogging Mattis's nose and throat until he stumbled backward. She reached out to grab him and was again caught off guard by Lorica, who flew in from behind, landing both of her feet on the Gigoran's back and taking them all to the ground.

If Ymmoss had been playing an aggressive Gigoran game earlier, now she was truly incensed. She thrashed at Mattis and Lorica wildly, clawing huge scratches in Mattis's chest. She tried to rise, but Lorica wrapped her arms around Ymmoss tightly and struggled to keep her in the mud where, perhaps, the chaos would give the Gigoran the disadvantage.

"Her—legs—" Lorica managed to grunt before Ymmoss belted her across the jaw. But to Lorica's credit, she held fast.

Mattis managed to follow directions and wrap

himself around Ymmoss's thrashing legs. Her knee pounded against his scratched chest, sending a blaze of pain throughout his torso that he could feel in the tips of his fingers, but he held on as Lorica again pressed herself into the Gigoran's matted fur and stroked Ymmoss's head. It was a strange way to fight, but it seemed to calm the Gigoran at least a little, though she did still kick out every few seconds, sending fresh bursts of pain through Mattis. Lorica's lips were moving, but Mattis couldn't make out what she was saying.

Then the shock came.

A bolt of electricity coursed through the Gigoran's body and then through Mattis's and Lorica's, too, rending them apart from each other. They landed heavily in the dirt, panting to catch their breaths. Ymmoss tried to stand against the purple current that danced about her, singeing her fur, and the guard holding the electrostaff pulsed her again. This time, the Gigoran fell face-first into the mud, then rolled onto her side, purring softly in pain, clutching her stomach against the diminishing current.

Lorica pulled herself to her knees. Her jaw was bruised from the Gigoran's punch. Her hair was caked to her face with mud, and her arms, where they weren't covered, were scraped. Mattis held his head just high enough from the ground to take her in, feeling a tiny whirlwind of anger and sorrow, of gratitude and remorse, before rolling himself over to a sitting position.

Once there, when he had caught his breath and the Fold around him came back into focus, only then did he recognize the guard who'd broken up their fight: it was AG-90, polished to a new sheen, his chest plate baring the unmistakable insignia of the First Order.

CHAPTER
06

"WE NEED TO GO somewhere!" Sari yelled in Dec's ear. Dec wasn't as strong a pilot as AG-90, but he'd done enough hunting and trapping from his modified speeder bike back on Ques to deal with distractions while he piloted.

"We *are* going somewhere!" he hollered back.

It was unlike Sari to shout. It was unlike Dec to reply unkindly. They weren't acting like themselves. But in fairness, they were being pursued by First Order shuttles through a ring of detritus that circled the swamp planet below.

"Where? You're just dodging space junk," Sari

reasoned. She was back to her usual low tone and volume.

"You have to stop yelling at me," Dec said, unable to resist making the joke. He banked their shuttle hard to avoid some rather mean-looking debris.

"Dec." Sari rested her hand on his shoulder. "We have to get away from here."

Was she telling him to save their own lives, to leave the others on Vodran with the First Order? Dec wouldn't. And Sari ought to know that he wouldn't.

"I won't leave 'em, Sari," he said. "I'm not leaving our friends. My brother," Dec said with what he hoped was finality.

"Great. Perfect. All we need to do is evade the First Order on our tails and avoid the space junk all around us," Sari complained. "*And* conserve enough fuel to get us back to Vodran to save them from who knows what. This would be easier if we had artillery."

"Look on the bright side," Dec told her. "The First Order shuttles must not have artillery, either, or we wouldn't even be in this jam." Dec smiled and banked the shuttle again, just avoiding half a discarded skiff floating along inconveniently.

"Dec, do something," Sari said.

Dec nodded. He could outmaneuver these wing-dings. He'd dodged drift bark on the swamps of Ques since he was five years old. Dec flew the shuttle over and through the debris, which stretched into a long belt of metal and other refuse across the curve of the planet below.

"I'm gonna get closer to some of this stuff," Dec told Sari. "Hold on to something."

Sari already looked pretty green. She fell back into one of the passenger seats and strapped herself in, tugging the flimsy belt across her massive body.

Dec bore toward a spinning piece of metal just ahead of them. His brother would've slipped over and around that hunk of debris with ease and flair. Dec knew he could do it, but the best he could hope for was minor damage to their own shuttle and the chance that one of their pursuers would hit it. When he should have slowed down, Dec gunned the shuttle's engines and flew within meters of the spinning wreckage. A jagged edge came up and ground against his ship. Dec pulled abruptly upward, turning and spinning the shuttle as smaller debris buffeted the cockpit, sparking and chafing the glass.

Behind and below, their closest pursuer wasn't so lucky. The First Order shuttle didn't pull up as Dec had done, and the spiked metal junk sliced raggedly through it. Its pilot floated off into space, and what remained of his ship joined the rest of the wreckage in dangerous orbit.

"Dec, what's that?" Sari leaned forward in her seat, squinting through the viewport.

"More junk, probably," Dec said, flipping switches and turning dials on his flight controls while attempting to avoid any more close calls but still keep the two remaining shuttles off his back.

"No, look," she demanded.

"Kinda busy right now, pal," Dec replied.

"Dec! Look out!"

Dec was so busy staring down at his flight screens that he barely noticed the small moon into whose orbit they were flying. Their shuttle juddered and banked as they flew into the moon's gravitational sphere, and Dec pulled hard on his controls. They shot down into the moon's clouded atmosphere. Behind them, one of their pursuing ships lost control and, unable to compensate for the moon's gravity or its sudden entry, spun front to back over and over, then plummeted to the surface. No one could have survived the crash.

The other First Order ship lost them in the clouds. For the moment.

It was another minute before Dec fully regained control and they could take in their surroundings.

"What is this?" Dec asked.

"It's a moon," Sari told him.

"Not one of Vodran's," he said. "This moon, if it is one, didn't show up on scans." Dec took in the heavy, low cloud cover and the empty green swathes of land below. "Why didn't it show up on scans, Sari?"

Sari shrugged. "Could be any number of things," she said. "Could be a naturally occurring phenomenon. Like some mineral deposits below its crust make it invisible to scans. Could be that someone is cloaking it somehow. I mean, I guess that technology is possible." She sounded more curious than fearful, though Dec thought it ought to be the other way around. But Sari had a scientific mind, and this invisible moon had piqued her interest.

The comm had stopped squawking since they had entered the moon's orbit. Sari studied it, intrigued, then turned back to Dec.

"Look," she said, sensing his apprehension,

"we ditched two of those First Order scouts, but that other one knows we're here. He followed us down here. Whatever is masking the moon from outside scans also makes communication from its orbit impossible. Comm channel is quiet, right? That's a good thing. He can't signal Vodran that we're here."

"Unless he turns around and leaves the moon."

"But then he risks losing us altogether. Scans don't work here due to whatever is blocking the moon itself."

"What're you getting at, Sari?"

"I'm saying this invisible moon is a good place to hide. Even if the First Order sends a whole squadron, they won't be able to find us until they literally fall into our laps."

Dec considered it. He didn't like the idea of cooling their heels on some ghost moon while his brother and their friends were down on Vodran.

"It's as good a plan as we have right now," Sari said. "We can stay here and regroup, at least. We won't be able to send out communications, but no one—First Order or Resistance—will be able to find us, either. And that's okay for now, isn't it?"

"We can't just fly in circles," Dec said, surveying

the visible stretches of land in front of him. What he could see through the low fog, anyway.

"No, we'll have to find somewhere to set down," Sari agreed. "Like there." She pointed to where a small gray bunker appeared, as if it had been dropped into a green pasture.

"What is it?"

"Only one way to find out. At least it isn't a First Order stronghold," Sari reasoned. "They'd never hole up in something so ugly."

Dec knew he was supposed to laugh, but he couldn't. He piloted the shuttle toward the bunker, knowing even as he did that it was a dangerous idea.

CHAPTER

07

"I'M HUNGRY." It was the first thing Lorica had said to Mattis in hours.

After AG-90, now a First Order guard droid, broke up their fight in the Fold, he'd escorted Mattis, Lorica, and Cost back to their cell and left them to stew. That's what he'd said. "Stew over what you did." It was and it wasn't the kind of thing the old AG might say. There was something different about his voice and the way he carried himself. Not to mention the First Order insignia on his chest plate. But "stew over what you did." Mattis just didn't know what to make of that. He wanted to talk to Lorica about it, but upon arriving at their cell, she slumped in her bunk with her arms crossed. A stormtrooper eventually brought in antiseptic wipes and some gauze dressings, the latter of which did not look sterile at all. But they did the job of mopping up the blood that had crusted on their wounds, and though he was still a bit wobbly from the electro-shock AG had given them, Mattis did feel better once he'd cleaned himself up. At least he wasn't finding Gigoran fur in uncomfortable places.

"I'm hungry, too," Mattis said, realizing as he said it that it was true.

Lorica glared at him.

"Hey," Mattis said with more anger in his tone than he'd intended, but then he *was* hungry, and that was making him cranky. "I didn't start that fight."

"You didn't finish it, either," Lorica huffed.

"Neither did you! Aygee did. Our friend. He electro-shocked us!"

"Doesn't look like he's our friend anymore," Lorica said with venom.

"No, it doesn't," Mattis agreed angrily. "Don't you think we should talk about that?"

"Why? It's obviously too late. They got him. They got Jo. Who do you think is next?" She raised an eyebrow, implying that it wouldn't be her.

"That Gigoran did not like you, for starters!" Cost chirped from her perch above Lorica, then peeled into loud, sharp laughter.

"Hey, c'mon," Mattis said. "That's not fair. I didn't do anything!"

"You *actually* didn't do anything," Lorica agreed. "You barely got out of the way."

Mattis didn't think that was true. He thought that, faced with a rampaging Gigoran, he had done just about enough—which was, sure, very little. But he didn't get his face clawed off, either, so he considered himself successful.

Mattis let out a long sigh, signaling to Lorica that he didn't want to say what he was about to say. But that was a show, of course. He was happy that they were talking. "Thanks for saving me," he said.

"What else was I gonna do?" she responded. Her cool response was undermined when her stomach rumbled irritably. "I'm so hungry," she complained.

"They have to feed us eventually, right?" Mattis reasoned.

Cost hopped down off her bunk and started her pacing ritual. Back and forth she went, flapping her arms and running them up and down along the back wall. "Do you hear it?" she asked. When they didn't respond, she repeated, "Do you hear it? Do you hear it?" Her perseverance made Mattis wish he'd had his ears ripped off by the Gigoran.

"They can do whatever they want, Mattis," Lorica said sharply. "We're their prisoners."

"But they want information, right?"

"They probably already have it! They reprogrammed Aygee, so maybe they got whatever he had out of him before they did that. And Jo—like you said, he doesn't care about us."

"Did I say that?"

"You said he turned. Or that he was never one of us at all. Same thing. I'm sure he told them everything by now."

"Do you hear it? Do you hear it?" Cost's refrain grew louder and faster. *"Doyouhearit? Doyouhearit?"*

"Cost, shut up!" Lorica spat, and cursed their cellmate in Zeltron.

"Well, maybe he didn't!" Mattis shouted. Somehow he'd wound up in the odd position of defending Jo. Maybe it was the hunger that was making his mind as weak as his body.

"Let's pretend he did," Lorica snapped. "It's what you were trying to tell me before. So let's just say they know everything that we know. Which isn't much, is it?"

"I know some things," Mattis countered, annoyed.

"You don't know anything. You don't even know where the Resistance base is."

"You don't, either!"

"The scritching-scratching! It's in the walls, friendies. It's in the walls." Cost pounded on the walls with her little fists and yelled, *"Doyouhearit? Doyouhearit?"*

"I know more than you do!" Lorica stood now, bumping her head on the upper bunk, swearing again. *"Cotoogi,* Mattis!" she yelled.

"Don't get mad at me!" Mattis shouted. If they were going to continue this fight, then yelling was their best option to hear one another over Cost's carrying on.

"Scritching! Scratching!"

"Who else am I going to get mad at?"

"Yourself? Your boyfriend, Jo?"

"For the last time, Jo isn't my boyfriend. And anyway, we wouldn't even be on this stinkplanet if it weren't for *your* boyfriend, Dec!"

"Dec isn't my boyfriend!" Mattis didn't even know what they were arguing about anymore.

"Of course not. If he cared about you at all, he'd have turned his shuttle around and come to find us. But he didn't. He and that oaf Sari just took off."

"Well at least—at least—"

"At least what?"

They were in each other's faces, ready to come to blows. Mattis wouldn't make the first move, and he hoped Lorica wouldn't, either. She would definitely win a physical altercation against him. Heck, she'd nearly beaten that Gigoran.

"So loud in my ears! So loud in the walls!" Cost moaned and rocked in her corner.

"At least I'm a nice person!" Mattis finally yelled.

Lorica burst out laughing and gave him a shove. It wasn't at her full strength, he was sure, but then neither of them were. Still, it wasn't exactly a playful shove, and he fell back into his bunk, banging the back of his head on the overhead bar.

"Ow!"

"Just shut up already, Mr. Nice Person," Lorica growled.

"Make it stop, make it stop, make it stop so loud," Cost wailed.

"You shut up, too!" Lorica yelled into Cost's

corner, but Cost was back up again, pacing and running her thin fingers along the back wall.

"Quiet in there, prisoners!" AG's voice, though mechanical and missing his characteristic drawl, was still unmistakable. He appeared a moment later, standing ramrod straight before their cell door.

"Aygee," Mattis said, surprised. As he'd appeared in the Fold, AG seemed both himself and not himself. He was somehow more . . . mechanical. Over the course of knowing him, Mattis had come to think of AG-90 not just as a droid but as Dec's brother. As a friend. Mattis had ceased seeing any difference between himself and his friend. AG could think and act, and just like Mattis, he wanted to fly.

"That's me," AG said flatly. "You prisoners ought to stop yelling. You're liable to raise unwanted attention. You hear?"

Mattis nodded. He didn't like this new AG-90. He missed his friend.

"If you're not here to help us, then I don't know why you're here," Mattis said. He hoped he conveyed the disappointment he felt. He hoped it sliced through AG's programming.

The droid gave no indication that it had.

AG's presence had done one thing, though, and that was to further agitate Cost. She threw herself against the cell bars and grasped them so tightly that her knuckles turned white.

"Stop the noise!" she shouted in AG's faceplate. "It's noisome and *stop it, stop it, stop it!*"

"Step back, prisoner," AG ordered, but Cost went on barking and pleading for him to stop the noise, stop the scritching in the walls. "The scritching is in your brain, prisoner," AG said dryly.

Cost persisted, banging her fists on the bars, trying to shake them but finding herself unable. The bars were too strong. She stopped only when Ingo Salik made his imperious presence known by clearing his throat. He touched Cost's fingers where they held the bars, and she let go.

Cost turned to Lorica, standing beside her, and pointed. "She pet the Gigoran," Cost said.

Ingo offered a small, good-natured smile. "From the report I received, I don't think the Gigoran was too pleased by it."

"She tried to eat me. The Gigoran, I mean," Mattis told Ingo.

"Don't be silly. Gigorans don't eat people," Ingo remarked, then added mockingly, "usually."

"Could you blame her?" Lorica asked, stepping toward the bars, standing within a meter of Ingo. "It's not like we get fed in this cage."

Mattis didn't think that challenging their jailer was a good way to curry favor, but Ingo's features softened as Lorica locked eyes with him. There was something about Lorica, even when she was antagonistic, that made a person want to engage with her. Maybe even moreso when she was being antagonistic, which was her default manner anyway.

"Have you not been fed?" Ingo asked. The way he said it made them sound like chickens in a coop, which was probably his intention. "That's our error, Miss Demaris."

"So you know my name," Lorica remarked.

Ingo only nodded and maintained his thin smile. It took Mattis a moment to get to where Lorica already stood. Ingo hadn't known their names when last he visited them. Now he did. Which meant that Ingo, and his commander, Wanten, had received information from someone. Maybe AG, before he was reprogrammed, or more likely, Jo was reporting to the First Order. For now, as far as they knew, it was just their names. But what would come next? Mattis was sure AG didn't know the location of the Resistance base, but Jo, as squadron leader, probably did. Lorica had implied as much, and that was dangerous knowledge to have under capture.

Lorica took a step forward. Any closer and her nose would poke through the bars. But now she was a breath away from Ingo. Mattis was so worried about this confrontation he felt as if his head were going to jump off his neck. His pulse reached a crescendo and, suddenly, everything stopped being so dire. It was as if Mattis had spent all of his worrying and had just completely run out of concern. Everything moved slowly and placidly, as if underwater. As Ingo reached into his jacket pocket, Mattis didn't even tense. Everything was just so calm. Lorica remained nose to nose with Ingo, on opposite sides of the bars. Ingo removed a small rectangular foil-wrapped packet. Cost quieted to a soft humming.

Ingo lifted the packet to eye level and placed it on the bar between his and Lorica's faces. He held on to one end of it. Languidly, Lorica raised her own hand and took the other end. They remained there for a moment, each touching one end of the silver packet, then Lorica grasped it tighter and snatched the whole packet into her hand. She

took a step back from the bars, and whatever spell they'd fallen under was broken. The world moved at normal speed again. His head spinning, Mattis dropped back onto his bunk.

Ingo nodded, stepped back, turned on his boot heel, and exited the way he had come.

Lorica turned to Mattis, her eyes wide. She ripped open the silver packet to reveal six gelatinous cubes.

"Is that—" Mattis began, unable to believe his own eyes. His stomach finished the question for him.

Lorica nodded. She still seemed dazed from whatever hocus-pocus had just transpired, as if she could feel it, too, and why not? She was just as spent as Mattis was.

"It's a ration pack," she said. She broke off three of the cubes and tossed them to Mattis. "Eat," she said.

Mattis gulped one down without even tasting it, which was probably for the best. The protein cubes that came in ration packs were notoriously sickly sweet, like eating sugar boiled in hawkey nectar. Which was to say cloyingly sweet. He felt the nutrients jolt him with energy before the cube was even all the way down his throat.

Lorica held her first cube on her tongue, clearly not minding the syrupy sweetness, savoring the rush of energy she got from finally consuming some food.

Mattis went to place a second cube in his mouth and then stopped. Cost rocked back and forth in the corner, one hand splayed up against the back wall, as if she could somehow keep it from falling in on her that way. She was drawn and skinny.

Mattis took one of his two remaining protein cubes and held it out to Cost. She only seemed to recognize what it was after a blink. Then she rose up unsteadily and Mattis placed the cube in her hand.

"Thanks a bucket," she said. She slipped the cube into her mouth like she was taking back a secret.

Lorica watched the transaction take place, sighed, and offered Cost one of her cubes as well. Cost took it and put it into her mouth with the other cube, which hadn't yet dissolved.

"Don't choke on it," Lorica said unhappily. Mattis could tell she'd wanted all three for herself. But she hadn't taken them. Indeed, she'd first given half her bounty to Mattis and then a third to Cost. They were together in this.

"Thank you," Mattis said to her. The words didn't contain the galaxy of gratitude he actually felt.

"Mm hmm." She nodded, the first cube still on her tongue.

"What did you—" Mattis began. He wasn't sure how to ask. He wasn't even sure what he was asking. "Did you do something to him?" It came out sounding accusatory and Mattis wished it hadn't.

"No!" Lorica was defensive.

"I didn't mean—I don't know the words," Mattis said. "But it's like . . . do you have the Force?" Something in the question surprised and disappointed Mattis. A part of him thought that if Lorica possessed the Force, it would mean he didn't. Of course, that was a ridiculous notion. In the days of the old stories, there were plenty of Force users.

"I don't," Lorica replied. "Because there's no such thing."

Mattis didn't think this was the time to argue, as much as he wanted to convince her of the truth.

"Then how did—" he began, unsure again how the question should be asked.

She sighed and crooked her mouth, as if this were something she'd given a great deal of thought. Which she had. "I've been realizing this for a while," Lorica said. "I think there's something about . . . me."

Mattis wanted to tell her that there were lots of things about her, things about which *he'd* given a great deal of thought, but for once, he thought it better to shut up and let her continue. This wasn't easy for her to explain.

"There are . . . rumors? Legends? I don't know. About my people, about Zeltron people. They say that we can sort of affect things, feelings, in others."

"Like mind control?" Mattis asked.

"Brain-itching!" yelled Cost.

Mattis went to shush her, but Lorica stopped him with a hand held up. "It kind of *is* like brain-itching."

"Brain-itching isn't a thing that anyone's heard of," Mattis pointed out.

"No," Lorica agreed. "I guess not. But it's, like, emotion massaging, if that makes sense."

"It doesn't."

"Mattis, don't get angry with me. I'm trying to explain."

Mattis apologized.

"They say that Zeltrons have these pheromones,

like, we radiate something—a smell or a feeling that makes people like us. I mean, more than we're already likable." She smiled at her own joke. "It has a calming effect on people. And Gigorans, apparently."

"That's why you were petting Ymmoss," Mattis said, understanding.

"Yeah," Lorica replied. "Being that close to her, and soothing her as I was, I think it calmed her down."

"A little bit, sure," Mattis agreed.

"Hey," Lorica snapped. "She's a Gigoran, and I'm new at this. But I think if I were better at it, if I practiced, I could put her to sleep."

"Is that what you did with Ingo?"

"Not exactly. I think . . ." She shook her head, though the notion didn't embarrass her at all. "I think he likes me. So I sort of . . . used that."

Mattis nodded. It made sense. Ingo hadn't had his mind controlled by Lorica, but that haze he'd been in was real. He knew what he was doing, giving her the ration packet. Part of him wanted to give it to her. But Lorica's ability had pushed him so that he didn't mind actually doing it.

Mattis thought back to his own interactions

with Lorica, from the time they'd met on the transport to the Resistance base. She hadn't been nice to him, but he'd been drawn to her nonetheless. And over time, as they got to know each other, he'd seen beneath the thorny front she presented to the good person who was inside of her. She'd saved him, and Dec and AG and the others, many times. And every time she did—well, really, every time she did anything—Mattis liked her a little bit more. He saw where that affection was going; he'd felt the same for his pal Jinby back on Durkteel, though he'd resisted it and they'd remained just friends. It wouldn't help to get a crush on someone who was his friend and, often, his sparring partner. But his feelings were as strong and undeniable as the Force itself.

This new information rankled him. If just being near her enhanced every feeling Mattis had, then were his feelings for her real? Were they even friends? Or was she just itching his brain to make her life easier? Did it make any difference that she'd only recently realized she had these abilities? And was it even true? Mattis didn't want to explore those questions, and he pushed down any feelings that were simmering. After all, he didn't need Lorica making them worse. He'd wait until they had some time to themselves, and then maybe he could figure out how he actually felt.

Of course, time to himself seemed unlikely in their cramped cell.

"You're mad," Lorica said to him.

"I'm not mad," Mattis said, sounding very mad.

"I'm not mad, either!" Cost piped up.

"I don't care if you're mad," Lorica told her.

"You should." Cost hiccuped. "When I'm mad, I get angry."

Lorica shook her head. Mattis could tell that she didn't want to have the conversation, either. She was, as she often was, all business. He met her eye, if only for a moment. "We can use this, this ability I have, to escape."

"How?" Mattis huffed.

"I got Ingo to give me the rations packet, didn't I?" She cocked her head at him. He could tell that she needed him to listen and to under-stand the sense of what she was saying, but he was having trouble concentrating, as he usually did when she was around. With this new information, zeroing in on an idea was difficult. "Maybe I can get him to let us go," Lorica continued.

Mattis stared at her through slitted eyes. "How

are you going to make him want to let us go? Are you going to get him to fall in love with you?"

"No! I'll get him to see me as a person, instead of as a prisoner," Lorica barked.

"Okay. When?" He crossed his arms.

She shook her head at him. "I don't know when," she sighed. "I don't even know if it'll work. I can at least try. That's more than you're doing, sulking."

They were fighting again. Mattis didn't mind so much this time.

"I'm doing something, too."

"What are you doing?"

"I've been thinking of a plan since I got here," he said, omitting "or trying to" from the end of the statement.

"What have you got so far?"

And then, all at once and just at that moment, Mattis thought of a plan. He hoped it was due to having been trying to think of one since he got there. He would accept that maybe the Force had just then whispered a plan to his brain. He hoped it wasn't Lorica itching an idea into his head.

"I'm collecting scraps."

Lorica shot a question at him with a hard look.

"Like what we're doing on Vodran in the first

place, right? Maybe that's *my* special ability: the ability to find garbage."

"Mattis, what are you talking about?"

"They'll put us to work outside at some point," he said. "You saw some of the other prisoners out there, working on the fences and digging outside the Fold."

"I saw them."

"If we keep quiet, and if Aygee and Jo don't tell them everything just yet—"

"Which they already may have," Lorica pointed out.

"Maybe," Mattis agreed. "But then why keep us around?"

Lorica nodded. "Assuming we still have information they want, and they keep us around."

"They'll put us to work. This detention center is only half-completed. Wanten, the guy in charge, told me that. I'm sure I can find some scraps to use to get through this wall. Or under it."

"Can't go under!" Cost burst out. Both Mattis and Lorica shushed her. She whispered, "Can't go under. Gotta go through. Scritch-scratch!"

"Okay," Mattis said, humoring her. "I will. But Lorica, seriously, I'm sure I can find something to dig through. There's nothing on the other side of this wall but the open meadow that they caught us in."

"And probably a whole mess of stormtroopers ready to blast us."

"Maybe. But maybe we can outrun them. Maybe we can get a ship or a speeder bike or something and get out of here. It's worth a shot, isn't it?"

Lorica was quiet for a moment. "It is," she finally said. "Do it. Gather whatever you can find. Even if it's no good for digging and scraping away at the wall, maybe we can use what you find for weapons, if we need. Meanwhile, I'll work on my plan."

A part of Mattis wasn't eager to acknowledge that he recognized Lorica's plan to get Ingo on their side was a good one. If anyone could pull it off, she could. She was the most capable, toughest person he knew. A louder, more persistent part of him hoped she failed. He didn't want to see Ingo fall in love with her.

CHAPTER

08

"**I** HAVE A REALLY LOUSY feeling here," Dec told Sari as he brought their shuttle in for a landing by the gray bunker that sat in the middle of an expanse of deep dark green.

"You want to go back and face those First Order scouts? Or maybe go all the way back to Vodran and just hunt around for our friends until we get eaten by rancors or tawds or worse?" Sari responded, leaning over his shoulder to watch the ground grow closer beneath them.

"Nothing's worse than a tawd," Dec said, setting the shuttle down. He stood up. He was glad to be back on solid ground, anyway, even if they were facing the unknown. At the very least, maybe the bunker would have some fuel. They were low after all that evasive flying.

They packed some rations and hydration, as well as a stun rod they'd been given to ward off dianogas on Vodran, and walked down the boarding ramp into an eerie silence. Thick mist swirled around them, and they could barely make out the bunker in the near distance. There were no signs of life.

"Maybe it's abandoned," Sari reasoned.

"You think someone living by himself on an invisible moon in the Outer Rim is going to welcome us with a parade?" Dec replied.

"Good point, but now that you ask, that's what I'd vastly prefer." When Dec shot her a skeptical half scowl, Sari shrugged. "What? Parades are fun."

They took a few steps forward before Dec put away his flashlight. "Light's just bouncing off the mist," he said. "We're walking in blind."

"Okay," Sari said. Then, steeling herself, she added, "What's the worst we could find?"

As they moved toward the bunker, a large paneled door slid up. Through the haze, they couldn't see inside at all, but figures emerged from within. A gang of indistinct shapes, maybe a dozen of

them, moved eerily to intercept Dec and Sari. Dec set his stun rod to charge. It hummed softly. Sari clenched her hands into tight fists the size of young Ewoks' heads.

"What do you think?" asked Dec. "Guavian Death Gang?"

"Craygalon Marauders from Snowdn-4?" asked Sari.

"The Galgardi Syndicate?"

"Noreeno Horde?"

"Estipona Party Squad?"

Sari shot him a puzzled look. Dec explained, "They're cannibals."

"Oh."

Dec and Sari hunched in ready positions. Maybe they would die on this invisible moon, and no one would ever know what happened to them. That they died fighting. That they died together, great friends, defending each other to the end.

"The Mangan Ring?"

"Bloody Montantis?"

"Droids."

"Droids?"

"Look," she said, pointing. "They're droids."

"We can definitely fight droids," Dec said.

"They're droids." Sari shook her head, trying

to explain. "We probably won't have to fight them. How many territorial droids do you know? If they were sentries, they would have attacked already. No one sends a bunch of broken-down droids to fight. Do they?"

As the figures came more clearly into view, Dec saw that they *were* broken-down droids. A dozen of them, in various states of disrepair, all different classes and types. Some wobbly proto-col droids of different heights. A floating probe droid with only a few spindly legs remaining. An astromech stutter-rolled, stopped, then contin-ued toward them, emitting a low, prolonged tone. And more: a medical droid with half a head; a hulking construction droid; a lightweight naviga-tion droid whose right hand had been replaced with the dual laser cannons of a B2 battle droid. She must have been their leader, for she met Dec and Sari first, stopping a couple of meters from them and raising her cannons. Behind her, her droid cohorts softly beeped and booped, blinking their signal lights.

Dec put down his stun rod and raised his hands. "We don't want any trouble," he said.

Sari put her hands in the air, too, and nod-ded. "No trouble."

The navigation droid didn't lower her cannons, even when all the robots lifted their heads skyward. A dirty gray-and-white astromech droid buzzed close to Dec. It passed him and his stun rod was gone.

"I might need that," Dec said casually.

The B2 and the others all leveled their gazes at the interlopers. They moved forward again, surrounding Dec and Sari.

"What are they doing?" Dec asked. He was used to asking her things. Sari knew everything.

"Ask them," she answered.

"They don't seem real chatty."

The oddball collection of droids walked, rolled, and hovered closer and closer.

"Too close," Dec said, to no effect. He and Sari started pushing back, but the droids were solid. They wouldn't be moved. Sari lost her footing and stumbled but didn't fall; the droids around her were so tightly packed that they held her up. They held Dec just as firmly and started moving. As one, slowly, centimeter by centimeter, the droids pushed Dec and Sari along inside their metal cocoon, herding them toward the bunker.

"Let us out," Dec managed, but he didn't know which droid he was telling. Maybe all of them.

He felt his jacket pulled off him. He grasped for it, tugging at the sleeve as it was stripped from him, but the droids were too strong. His satchel slipped to the ground and they walked over it.

He bumped against Sari, and she put her arm around him.

"Let's go with them," she said. "We don't have a choice anyway."

They stopped resisting and allowed the droids to carry them toward the dark open mouth of the bunker.

Some of the mist had cleared, the sun was shining harder and brighter than it had been, and Dec and Sari watched as the nav droid trekked out about halfway to their shuttle and raised her cannons again. There was a thrum as she activated them and then two electric spitting sounds—*thoom! thoom!*—as she fired. Plasma shots struck Dec and Sari's shuttle and it exploded.

None of the droids moved against the thunderous noise or the hot fire that followed. Dec, catching Sari's look, read in it his own thoughts precisely: They were stuck there. They were doomed. Things could not get worse.

Then they got worse.

Dec and Sari heard it before they saw it: a

First Order scout shuttle descending outside the bunker where they'd just stood, where their smoldering wreck still remained. They saw the First Order pilot through the cockpit viewport, a stern-looking young man not much older than Dec himself.

The First Order shuttle touched down and the nav droid, now wearing Dec's jacket, walked out to meet it.

Dec touched his head. He'd scraped it on one of the droid's chassis during the pressed-in throng. It was bleeding. That was the least of his worries right then, though. The droids were about to turn him and Sari over to the First Order.

CHAPTER

09

THE DIFFERENCE BETWEEN wakefulness and sleep while he was a prisoner of the First Order on Vodran was, to Mattis, a negligible one. When the thick gray afternoon gave way to the inky darkness of night, Mattis lay on his mattress and stared at the springs of the bunk above him until it became too black to see even those. He listened to Cost's whining, which fell to muttering, then to a fitful series of inhalations and exhalations as she dropped deeper into slumber. Across from him, Lorica was silent, only occasionally turning, growing annoyed in her sleep that she couldn't find a comfortable position, then accepting her sorry state and returning to stillness.

Mattis heard all this for hours and hours until he finally drifted off to a poor approximation of sleep. It was never restful. Any sound, even from far away, woke Mattis with a start. He lived in an ever-present state of alarm, always at the ready, always prepared to fight or flee. It wouldn't surprise him to wake one night to find the enraged Gigoran Ymmoss standing over him, her gargantuan paws ready to smother him or claw him to shreds. Nor would it astound him if Lorica jogged him awake to tell him it was time to go, that her plan had worked, that Ingo would free them, and all she had to do was promise Ingo her hand in marriage. His dread upon waking, Mattis both understood and feared, would be the same for either situation, and he dwelled upon both in his thoughts day in and day out. Occasionally, another notion surfaced: that he would celebrate birthday upon birthday, growing frail and gray-haired, in this detention center—first under Wanten's irked command and then under Ingo's more genial despotism. In that nightmare reverie, Lorica turned to the First Order and became Ingo's paramour, the two of them—and sometimes Jo and AG, too—tyrannical in their treatment of the prisoners and of Mattis in particular.

And then, once in a rare while, Mattis allowed himself to hope. He thought, as he'd done upon first arriving at the detention center, of General Leia. He might even smile in those times, albeit briefly. He allowed himself to think of Dec and Sari and the possibility that they *had* escaped Vodran and would return for their friends.

It was Dec and Sari, arriving in their shuttle, animated by adventures of their own, that Mattis dreamed of now as the real-world sounds of his cellmates grew abstract and his friends' arrival felt true. It was in this moment that thin fingers touched his shoulder and he jerked to a sitting position, throwing out his arms and, in the process, shoving Cost sprawling onto the floor.

"Hey!" Cost said.

"Shut up," Lorica said. There was no sleep in her voice.

"Sorry," Mattis said. "Cost woke me."

"Don't care," Lorica groaned. Mattis heard her bedsprings complain as she rolled away from them.

It was too dark to see whether Cost had returned to her bed, but Mattis assumed she had. She hadn't. Mattis felt those fingers return to his shoulder, pressing insistently.

"Hey! Are you awake now?"

He could just make out the shape of her kneeling beside him.

"Now, yeah," he said.

"I don't hear the scritching," Cost told him.

"Good," Mattis said, willing her away. "That's good, Cost. Get some sleep."

"Do you hear it?"

Mattis sat up in his bunk. Cost scrambled up, too, as if invited, and sat across from him with her legs crossed under her. Mattis cocked his head and listened for the scratching in the walls that he knew wasn't there.

"I don't hear anything," he told her.

"Then it won't hear us, either," she said, nodding, confident.

"Is something wrong, Cost?" Mattis asked. He really wanted to ask if something was right. Mattis couldn't remember Cost being quite so lucid in the time he'd known her.

"Everything's wrong," she whispered. She sounded haunted.

"Did you find something out? Did Ingo or one of the stormtroopers say something?" Mattis started to panic.

"I know some things," Cost said.

"What do you know?" Mattis asked desperately. His voice was rising, and now Cost shushed him. A first.

"I know that there are things in this universe beyond us," she said. "There are things beyond our understanding."

"I see," Mattis said, emitting a heavy sigh of relief. Cost wasn't talking about anything happening at the detention center. No one was coming for them. She was talking about philosophy. She was talking about religion. She'd gotten to thinking about her place in the galaxy and the meaning of life itself. She was talking about the Force.

"You don't understand," Cost insisted.

"You're talking about the Force. The energy created by all living things. It brings us together. Us, the galaxy, everything." Mattis recited concepts he'd learned in his Phirmist temple back on Durkteel and ideas he'd gathered from the old stories he collected.

"You're stupid," Cost told him.

"I'm not! That's what the Force is."

"Not talking about any Force."

Mattis felt he had to explain and defend himself. "Cost, the Force is the oldest and most powerful energy in the galaxy. In any galaxy!"

"Shhh!"

"Sorry. It's just—there's nothing else. If you're talking about something overwhelming and ancient, *that's* the Force. If you're talking about things beyond understanding . . . well, most people don't understand the Force. Except for Jedi." He didn't add that *he* understood the Force. That it was with him and that, someday, he'd have the opportunity to explore it fully. If he ever got out of this cell.

"Oh . . ." Cost said. Mattis saw her nodding in the dark. "Okay. You're stupid."

"Stop calling me stupid!"

"Stop being stupid!" she whisper-yelled. "And *shhh!*"

"Cost, if you don't mean the Force, please tell me what you're talking about." Mattis was exhausted. This conversation was wearing him out even more.

"I'm talking about evil," she said, her voice a thin whisper in the dark between them. A tremor climbed up and down Mattis's spine. "Evil, old and strong. You don't feel it in this place?" Cost shivered and inhaled sharply.

"I don't feel it," Mattis admitted. It was true. In this place, he felt afraid, he felt alone, he felt helpless and chilled to the bone, despite the planet's crushing humidity. But he didn't sense anything in the way that Cost was talking about. "What do you mean?" he asked.

"You know what this place used to be?"

"Harra the Hutt's stronghold," he said.

"Big mouths, stubby arms, big fat worms," Cost said.

"I know what Hutts are."

"The Hutt was mean."

"All Hutts are mean."

"Not all," Cost said innocently. "But Harra was mean. Wookiee-who-had-her-lunch-stolen kind of mean."

Mattis remembered the menagerie that Harra the Hutt had collected on this planet, the angry creatures who'd chased them down, the rancors who'd eaten Klimo. Those were pets for only the cruelest sort of being. Harra the Hutt must have been mean to trade in those creatures.

"You know what these boxes were?" Cost asked.

"You mean these cells?"

Cost nodded.

Mattis shrugged. "I guess I didn't think about it."

"These boxes were the Hutt's torture pits."

Again, that tremor wracked Mattis. But wait . . . it didn't make sense. "These aren't pits," he told Cost. "They're rooms. These were probably storage facilities."

Cost laughed humorlessly. "Pit isn't always a pit," she explained. "Hutt kept her enemies in these cages, didn't feed them, sent her guards in to torture and to torment."

"Cost, were you here then? When this was Harra the Hutt's palace? Were you in the torture pits?" Mattis felt his stomach lurch. If Cost had suffered under Harra the Hutt, that would explain her loose grip on reality.

"Cost was here. Cost is still here!" She patted his knee. "I'm tougher than any Hutt," she told him. "I can stand it. The scritching and scratching, the muttering and complaining of the devil in the walls."

There she went again. The devil in the walls.

"You don't believe," Cost said. "But believe, Mattis. This place isn't just walls and bars. This place has scars. It remembers the evils done here over many years. They imprint on the structure, in its bones."

"But you're tough," Mattis said, hoping to help

Cost from the emotional well into which she was lowering herself.

"I *am* tough. But this place . . . it makes you forget hope. It makes you think you'll never leave. Do you think that sometimes?"

Mattis admitted he did.

"That's what the ghosts here do. That's what the haunts here do. They suck it out of you, out from your heart. First sucks away your hope, and then it chews up your mind. You have to hang on to your mind."

"I'm trying."

"Don't try. Do it. Do it, do it, do it. Because you don't want to hear the rasping, scraping thing in the walls. Once you hear that, then you know. Hope? Gone. Mind? Going, going."

Mattis clung to the edges of his mattress. He felt his face grow hot and clammy.

"Then, after all the scritching and scratching, you hear the laughter. Ha ha ha. So funny. The thing in there, the man in the walls, he thinks everything is a joke. But when you hear the laughing, Mattis, when you hear the laughing, that's when you're all done. Mind is gone. They could set you free that day. They could put you on a shuttle and send you back to your home, but you would still be here. You'd be a prisoner forever. Prisoner of Wanten, prisoner of Harra the Hutt, prisoner in your own mind."

Mattis choked out a question. "What can I do?"

"Hold on to hope. Find her and keep her."

"Hope?"

"She wants to fly away. She wants to be free of here, but you can't let her go. You need her. In here, you need her most of all. You lose her, you hear the scraping, you hear the walls yammering and calling you names, and then you hear it laugh at you. You don't want the walls to laugh at you."

"I don't," Mattis said seriously.

She took his hand. Her hands were dry and felt fragile, like kindling.

"Did you lose hope, Cost?" Mattis asked her. He was afraid of the answer, but the way she was talking was the most coherent he'd heard her since arriving there. Even if her words were confusing or abstract, she clearly meant them earnestly and was distressed.

"Harra the Hutt kept her creatures," she said.

"I've seen them. Up close."

"Not all of them." Cost stared through Mattis into the blackness behind him, maybe even through the wall, which was silent to her now. "Hutt took me from vacation. Snatched me out of camping site."

"You took a vacation on Vodran?"

"I fish for dianoga. They make good soups!"

Mattis shook his head. That couldn't possibly be true.

"Hutt's bad friends, the ones who hung around her palace and ate her food and teased her animals, they found me and brought me to her. They thought I would make her laugh. Or maybe I could work. I couldn't do either, though."

She sighed, remembering sadly. "Harra the Hutt loved her creatures and mostly she loved to watch them fight. When they wouldn't fight each other, she loved to watch others fight them. She made a Wookiee fight a rancor one time. Guess who won."

"I don't want to think about it."

"The rancor won by eating the Wookiee. It took longer than you'd think."

"Thanks," Mattis said sarcastically.

"You're welcome. It's not a heartwarming story," she admitted. "It's really not even a story. It's just something that happened that I saw. And it isn't the worst thing that I saw."

"Cost," Mattis said. "When you couldn't work and you couldn't make Harra the Hutt laugh, did she make you fight a rancor?"

"I could never fight a rancor," Cost said, as if Mattis were a fool for even asking. "I wouldn't win. I would lose. It would eat me for sure."

"I guess it's good you didn't have to fight a rancor, then."

Cost looked at Mattis as if he were dumb. "Yes," she said in a voice that told him he was as dumb as her look had suggested. "It's good that I didn't have to fight a rancor." She shook her head as if to flick away the stupidity in the air. "Harra the Hutt had another pet. A bulgy, clumpy jelly-thing. Sticky with tentacloids that grabbed and drank and drank. It liked my sadness and my fear and my lonely feelings."

Mattis started to say he was sorry, but Cost continued.

"It drank them up. It took away the things I knew. Mother and Father and Other on Genhu. They found me in the Hendo bushes when I was a sprout. Other's big hands scooped me up and brought me to their cottage. I used to be able to feel it, those hands, leaving the dry, dry air of the Hendo orchard for the cool of the cottage.

But no more. The feeling is gone. I know it is fact, I know I had Mother and Father and Other, but I don't know their faces, I don't feel them anymore.

"The beast took it all with his tentacles. Now I just walk through a sunken dream of them. Like finding a story on the images on a smashed vase. Bushes and someone hiding inside them, but I don't know if I'm hiding or seeking. A man with teeth on the outside. And Other's hand outstretched, but did I take it? And the purple sky and how wide open it all was. Then."

Cost shrugged and wiped her pointed nose with her filthy sleeve. Then she settled down into herself and said, "Anyway. I know I fished for dianoga. And I know they make good soup."

"When the First Order came . . ." Mattis began.

"When the First Order came," Cost continued, "they used big guns to make holes in the Hutt's throne room. Some of her bad ones got blasted away. Most ran. Some are here. Your friend, the pig man. He was one of her bads."

The Gamorrean who'd challenged Mattis in the Fold had been part of Harra the Hutt's entourage. Mattis wondered what other prisoners might have been with him and what that might mean for their intentions.

"First Order set all of the Hutt's creatures to run free. That was a good thing, I think. They built the fences, but the creatures come back. Hutt fed them, and they want easy foods again. So they come back and Wanten builds more fences and they knock them down and then Wanten builds more. But at least Wanten doesn't make prisoners fight creatures."

Cost was optimistic tonight.

"Why didn't you run, Cost?" Mattis asked.

"Where to go? Couldn't remember. The jelly-beast took it. So, Cost stayed. And then it all went away. The faces of Mother and Father and Other and the rest. All that remained were the bars, and the walls, and the cells. And then the walls got itchy and then they laughed and laughed and laughed."

Cost dropped her head and sniffled.

Mattis didn't know what to say to Cost, who'd lost everything she knew. Until he did. Because Mattis still had something to give him hope, and he could share that with her.

"Cost," he said, nudging her. She sat up again. "You know Lorica and I weren't here alone.

There was a group of us. Two of our friends got away. Dec and Sari are their names. Dec is my best friend. He's a good pilot, but what he's really good at is getting stuff done. Any situation, Dec can turn it over and over and figure it out."

As he talked about his missing friends, Mattis felt hope swell inside him, inflating like a balloon.

"And Sari is amazing. I think you'll love her. She's big and strong, so strong! She could probably even beat up Ymmoss! She's maybe the smartest person I know."

"You said Dec is clever." Cost was skeptical.

"He is. He's clever. It's different. Sari is *smart*. She knows all kinds of things about all kinds of things. She can work computers like no one I've ever seen. Like she can talk to them. And she knows about insects and birds and . . . just everything. She reads all the time."

"I want to meet this girl who talks to computers," Cost decided.

"You will. You will. They got away, Cost, I just know it. And they'd never just leave us here if there was even a bantha hair's chance that we're alive. And we are."

Cost looked at Mattis with puzzlement. "Then where are they?"

"I don't know. Maybe they're headed for a friendly planet so they can contact the Resistance. And the Resistance will come down here in their X-wings. Maybe they'll send the big guns, too, Poe Dameron and Snap Wexley and Black Two. What was his name? I forget, but him, too!"

"I hope they send those big guns," Cost agreed, angrily sizing up the walls of their cell.

"They will," Mattis told her. "I just know they will."

They sat there together a moment, nearly hearing the distant X-wing squadron approaching, believing in their hope and clinging to it because hope was all they had in that gray cage.

"Tell me more about the Resistance," Cost said after a spell of silence.

"Yeah, by all means, keep running your mouth." The voice came out of the darkness beyond the bars. Mattis looked in that direction, and when his eyes adjusted, he saw AG-90's glowing eyes and a glinting light coming off his plating.

"Aygee," Mattis gasped, starting off his bunk.

"Stay where you are, prisoner," AG commanded.

Mattis fell back stiffly.

"That's not your friend," Cost told him.

Mattis heard AG's servos whir as the droid shook his head. "This can be easy. You two can have a pajama party if you want, but keep it quiet. You make noise, you get the electrostaff. You try anything, you get the electrostaff. You open your mouths about anything, anything at all, you get the electrostaff. I like using it. Get me?"

Mattis nodded. His friend was gone. His years of personality, his tics and idiosyncrasies, all of the things that made AG himself were gone. He wasn't deep down somewhere in this droid, in some secret coding from which Mattis might rescue him with sentimental speeches or dramatic pleas. This was the new AG-90. Ruthless, callous, and nasty.

"I can't hear you, prisoner," AG said. A bright beam of light sliced through the bars into Mattis's bunk. He blinked against the harsh white.

Across the brief divide, Lorica sat up in her bunk, shielding her eyes. "What in the name of Ptak is going on?" she asked.

"I'm telling your bunkie to keep his trap shut. Goes for all of you."

"I was sleeping," Lorica spat. "So how was I gonna say anything?"

"It's a warning," Cost explained.

In the too-bright beam, Lorica glared at her. "I get it."

"Get it?" AG said, and swept his gaze across all of them. "Good. And get to sleep."

Cost lowered herself from Mattis's bunk and silently climbed back into her own. Mattis hoped she'd remember their talk and find comfort in what he'd said.

AG switched off his light and took a step away from them. Then, as if it was an afterthought, he turned back to face them and said, "Your friends? The ones who escaped this planet? They're dead."

Mattis felt his face rush hot and red. "You don't know that!" he shouted.

"What'd I say about making a racket?" AG said, lifting the electrostaff from its holster. It hummed as he charged it up. "And don't tell me what I know. I was in the communications center. I heard the call come through. Some of our scouts found your pals circling Vodran. Gave chase. First Order soldiers are good, prisoner. So your friends? Dead and gone on some moon."

AG charged down his weapon, replaced it in its holster, and turned away.

"Sleep on that," he said, and left them.

Mattis experienced a moment of disbelief.

He'd just told Cost that Dec and Sari would return for them. Against his will, he let out a whimper. But AG, the new AG, had no reason to lie. He probably *couldn't* lie; it would go against his programming. Which meant that his friends were gone, gone forever, and he was stuck there. Stuck forever.

In the thick silence of the cell, he suddenly heard the scratching. *Scritch-scritch-scritch.* Faint at first, then bolder and unmistakable. Scratching in the walls. Soon they would be laughing, too.

After a few days of trudging between their cell and the Fold, Mattis and Lorica were put on construction duties. In that time, neither Wanten nor Ingo nor any First Order personnel approached them for information about the Resistance. They seemed to just be prisoners now, like any of the others. Lorica sensed in Mattis an acceptance of his fate. She didn't like that the fight had gone out of him. *When the fight is lost, the fight is lost*, she recalled reading in a history book about war. She carried that sentence with her. You had to stay angry; you had to hold on to the fight. If you didn't, where could you get the energy to go on?

Talking about feelings wasn't Lorica's strong

suit. Having them and tapping into them in others was. So, when she noticed the change in Mattis, she tried to draw him out. One morning—she thought it was morning, anyway, since the haze that surrounded their cell was a lighter gray than it was when they slept—Mattis was just staring at the corner of the room.

"What are you doing, Mattis?" she asked, trying to speak in her gentlest voice. He had been jumpy lately, like Cost had been when they'd first arrived.

At first he said nothing. She wasn't even sure if he'd heard her. But then he tilted his face to her, and she saw what he must have looked like when he was a little boy. "The scratching in the walls," he whispered.

"Mattis, that's not real."

Mattis shook his head. He appeared as if he hadn't slept in days. "I guess the good news is that when I go totally crazy, I won't have to worry about going crazy."

Lorica laughed. "That's a bad joke," she said.

"Yeah," Mattis said. The color didn't return to his cheeks, but something in his eyes made him look like his old, annoying, upbeat self, if only for an instant. "It's a bad joke," he agreed. "But it's a good truth."

"Mattis, you're not going crazy."

"I'm definitely not going sane, though."

He was keeping some version of a sense of humor, she thought, so that was a good sign. He wasn't all the way gone. She tried to keep him talking, asking him for stories about their brief time in the Resistance—something she knew he liked to think about—and the good things about growing up on Durkteel.

He responded, but every few minutes he'd sink back into that vacant hopelessness. At a certain point, Lorica abandoned the idea of letting Mattis share and just filled the room with words.

One day, when his gloom got to be too much altogether, she told him, "Snap out of it."

"There's nothing to snap out of," he replied.

She smacked him on the back of his head. They were slogging through the Fold on their way to the far side of the throne room to repair the hole that had been put there by the First Order when they'd initially arrived. It was their second day on the detail, and Mattis was terrible at it. Lorica had done the work of both of them, really. She'd made sure that the other prisoners who worked beside them didn't see just how small a load Mattis could carry with his skinny arms. She'd made sure that she did his work so the guards wouldn't notice his pathetic effort. At the end of the day, Lorica had been spent and aching.

"No physical contact," the stormtrooper escorting them barked. Lorica could see that he just wanted something to yell at them about.

"I can't do this forever," Lorica told Mattis.

"Too bad," he mumbled. "This is what we do now."

"Mattis, I mean it."

"So do I." He tripped over a stone, and she caught him. The stormtrooper was on them in a moment, yanking them apart.

"He tripped," Lorica complained.

"Don't care," the stormtrooper informed her.

"I'm okay," Mattis said, shaking it off.

"Also don't care," the stormtrooper said. "Keep walking."

They did, with their guard half a step behind them.

"Mattis, I'm not going to carry your load today," Lorica said. "I can't."

Mattis shrugged. "Okay."

She sighed impatiently and shook her head. Mattis was beyond help. He was resigned to remaining in the detention center for the rest of his life. Well, Lorica wasn't. She'd carry on with her plan. In a few days, she'd made some progress with Ingo. It was nothing like the moment they'd shared that first night, when he'd given her the rations packet, but his demeanor softened when he was in her presence. Whatever it was that Lorica possessed, whatever ability her Zeltron blood gave her, it appeared to work. There was even a marked difference in the way Ingo stood, from when he first approached their cell to when Lorica came closer to him. She could see his shoulders fall a little less square, the set of his chin become a little less harsh. For now, that small effect was enough. She would keep at it. She was certain she could get him to release them.

For now, she had to carry on. She'd let Mattis wallow, if that was what he needed to do, but she wouldn't encourage it and she wouldn't cover for him. That would only get her into trouble. She needed to avoid angering her keepers. That was the only way to succeed. That was the only way to survive.

When they arrived at the far throne room wall, Lorica took a moment to re-tie her boots while Mattis stared gloomily into the sky. She remained resolute: she wouldn't help him again.

While the other prisoners—the Gamorrean who'd been part of Harra the Hutt's coterie, a Pau'an with a large scar across his high forehead, a Flann with his timbered heart exposed—retrieved their tools and deliberately got to work, Mattis shuffled around in small circles. He kicked at plants and bugs and rocks and things and didn't do much to make himself look busy. He clearly didn't care. Lorica knew that Mattis figured it made no difference if he worked on repairing the wall or didn't; he was still stuck there.

A couple of their stormtrooper guards put their helmets together and talked quietly, motioning to Mattis. He couldn't be bothered to change what he was doing, so he just kicked another rock down the hill behind him to the pile of bigger rocks that was down there. It made a satisfying knocking sound when it landed.

"Hey, prisoner," one of the two stormtroopers hailed him. Mattis didn't stop his shuffling rotation, so the stormtrooper, annoyed, had to go over to where he was. He put a hard armored hand on Mattis's shoulder to stop him from moving. "You can't do this work?" the guard asked.

"I actually really can't do this work." Mattis pointed to the beefy Gamorrean. "That guy is like ten times my size, and he's struggling to haul that lumber." The Gamorrean shot Mattis a look and snorted. Mattis pointed to the Flann. "That guy is literally made of trees. He's crazy strong."

"You're asking for an easier detail?" the stormtrooper asked.

Nearby, Lorica listened to the conversation. She hoped Mattis wouldn't say anything stupid but knew that he probably would.

"I'm asking to go back to my cell so I can go to sleep."

Yep, he'd said something stupid.

"You don't seem to understand your role here," the stormtrooper said. "Your job is to do as you're told."

"Or else what?" Mattis asked. "You'll lock me up?"

This took the stormtrooper aback, and he looked over to his companion—Mattis couldn't tell if it was in disbelief or for assistance. The other stormtrooper, the one Mattis called Patch, approached. As he passed Lorica, she tensed, her instinct to trip the stormtrooper very strong. But she didn't. Mattis was on his own.

Lorica knew all this wasn't going to end well for Mattis.

CHAPTER

10

IT ENDED BETTER for Mattis than Mattis had anticipated. He knew he shouldn't have been kicking rocks and pouting about his work detail. He caught all the warning looks Lorica was throwing at him, but he couldn't help himself. He was so far in the dumps that all he could see was the bottom of the dumps. And no one wants to spend his days looking at dumps-bottoms.

So when Patch approached, all commanding attitude and clipped questions, Mattis just knew he was going to make the mistake of giving his guards some lip. "What's the problem here?" Patch asked.

"This prisoner doesn't like his detail."

"My guess?" Mattis said, sounding more to himself like his old friend Dec the more he talked back to these guards. "Nobody likes their work details. It's muggy and sticky and hotter than two suns smushed together out here." It was like Mattis was channeling Dec's dislike of authority figures. He missed his friend so much.

"Two suns smushed together wouldn't be any hotter than two individual suns," Patch said. Mattis was pretty sure the stormtrooper wasn't making a joke. Did stormtroopers even know how to make jokes? Was it against their protocol?

"Get back to work," the other stormtrooper said irritably.

Mattis didn't know what overcame him, whether it was the heat or the misery, but instead of picking up a tool, he just dropped onto the ground and sat. He was sorry when he did it, not only because it was bound to anger the stormtroopers, but also because the ground was wet and muddy.

Still, it made Lorica laugh, so that was something.

"That's it," Patch the stormtrooper said. "Separate these two. Give the smart guy another detail. Send him out to the perimeter."

"Are we authorized to make that decision?" the first stormtrooper asked.

"*I'm* authorizing it," Patch answered. "Ingo told us to solve problems. So, I'm solving this problem." The stormtrooper looked down at Mattis. "With any luck, he'll be eaten by a tawd before anyone even notices we've moved him."

Two days later, Mattis had a new detail. The perimeter fence on the outside of the palace's spread needed constant repair. It was frequently torn apart by rancors returning to the palace for food, which they'd once been given in abundant supply, as if they were pets of Harra the Hutt. Which they kind of were.

Mattis's job was to walk the length of the fence every day, flagging areas that needed repair. It was, by turns, tedious and dangerous. The walk took over an hour. When he completed the circuit, he was meant to begin again. After all, something might have damaged the fence while he was on the opposite side of the palace. Mattis spent all day literally walking in circles on a hike that might be interrupted at any moment by a throng of tawds or a pack of rancors.

He was allowed to carry a weld-bar on his

walks, which would do absolutely nothing against any animal attack. Still, the weight of it was comforting in his hands, as if he actually had a chance.

Mattis wasn't expected to repair the fence himself. It had been made clear that Mattis couldn't be trusted with tools, nor was he likely clever enough to fix anything. So, on his daily rotation, he was joined by Patch. Patch was armed with an FWMB-10 repeating blaster, a weapon favored by stormtroopers. Patch had modified his blaster for more power in case of an attack, though Mattis doubted it would do much to a rancor's thick hide other than slow the creature down. But the FWMB-10 also accomplished the task of intimidating Mattis.

As if one stormtrooper guard wasn't enough, Mattis was also guarded by Jo, who led the group on its march around the compound. Jo now wore a stiff First Order uniform. He carried himself in the same way he always had, aloof and superior. Upon seeing him on his first day of the detail, Mattis's jaw had dropped and he'd been about to speak or yell or complain or ask his former friend a question, but Jo had shut him down with just a look. Other than that, he hadn't done more than bark the occasional order or point out some break in the fencing. Another friend lost.

The final companion on these day-long treks was Ymmoss, the Gigoran. The memory of her attack on his first day in the detention center didn't do much to ease Mattis's anxiety.

Their first day on perimeter detail, Ymmoss had knocked through Patch and Jo and come after Mattis with swinging paws. Mattis was glad to have his weld-bar that day. He swung it at the Gigoran and even hung on to it when Ymmoss tried to knock it from his hands. Mattis got in a couple of solid defensive blows, too, and he was proud of himself. The fight ended when the powerful Gigoran pulled Mattis's weapon from his grip. He watched the weld-bar get flung to the ground and then found himself following it there. Ymmoss stood over him, bellowing. Mattis was saved when Patch hit Ymmoss with the shock-stick. The jolt she took would have made a happabore roll over, but Gigorans were uncommonly sturdy. There hadn't been any incidents with Ymmoss since then, but Patch mostly stayed between them. If Mattis caught her eye, Ymmoss gave an angry snarl.

Mattis wished Ymmoss would realize that they

were in the same boat. Both of them were prisoners on Vodran. Both of them were enemies of the First Order. He wished Ymmoss had a little more empathy and a lot less rage.

He also wished that he could take that weld-bar back to his cell with him after his detail finished each day. Its long body and spade-shaped grabber at the end would be perfect for chipping away at the concrete cell wall. If he could get through that, he could dig an escape tunnel. It might take years, even with a tool so solid, but at least he'd be free. But the weld-bar was collected by Jo at the end of every day like a ritual. Mattis handed the bar to Jo, who quickly inspected it (for what, Mattis couldn't figure), and then Jo passed the tool over to Patch, who stowed it in his pack. The same was done with Ymmoss's tools. The prisoners were then marched back to their cells.

Every night, Mattis lay awake listening to the scratching in the walls, fearing it would turn to laughter. It hadn't yet, but he grew more despondent as the nights wore on.

After a few days, Mattis rediscovered hope. It came in the form of a stubbed toe and a tarnished hunk of heavy junk.

Where most might hang their heads in despair, Mattis's depression left him with a tendency to tip his face skyward and get lost in the slate of gray clouds that were omnipresent over Vodran. He often needed reminding that while he trudged along the perimeter fence he was meant to do a job. Jo usually did that prodding, sometimes literally, poking Mattis in the chest or arm when Mattis drifted too far into space and missed some section of the fence that wanted repair. When this happened, Ymmoss would let out a gurgling growl-laugh and Patch would say something like, "Why bother with this kid?" Jo ignored them but made it clear to Mattis that he ought to do better.

Mattis was too tired and too forlorn. So the pattern repeated, and he was lucky that he didn't trip over the bramble or construction rubble that still scattered the detention center property. Until he did.

"Ow!" Mattis took a few stumbling steps then plopped down in the mud, holding his foot in his hand.

"Get up, prisoner," Patch said, and prodded Mattis with the nose of his gun.

"What happened?" Jo asked, annoyed.

"I wasn't looking where I was going," Mattis admitted.

Ymmoss groaned.

"I know, I know," Mattis replied, even though he couldn't understand the Gigoran.

"Can you walk?" Jo asked in a way that sounded more like an order than a question.

Mattis scowled at him. "Of course I can walk. Can you not act like a jerk?" It was sweaty and muggy out there, and though Mattis knew it was a bad idea to mouth off to Jo—even before finding out his so-called friend was a First Order flunky—sometimes he couldn't help himself. It was that little piece of Dec that he kept inside of him.

"Can you not act like a whiny baby tauntaun?" Jo shot back at him.

"Baby tauntauns don't whine," Mattis corrected. "They bleat."

"I'm gonna bleat you if you don't shut up and keep walking."

The silly pun almost made Mattis laugh, but the threat wasn't lost on him.

Mattis gave his big toe another rub, then stood and scanned the ground for whatever he had tripped over. He didn't see anything, and figured it was a small branch or maybe a tawd bone that had fallen from a rancor's mouth, so he continued on his detail, stopping every so often to massage his foot, to the exasperation of all three of his attendants.

It was a couple of hours before they completed the circuit again and Mattis found himself back in the spot where he'd stubbed his toe. He didn't realize it, of course. He was, again, staring into the sky, thinking how nice it would be if it rained. It always seemed about to rain on Vodran but rarely did. If it rained, Mattis thought, certainly his minders would return him to his cell, where he might see Lorica, possibly even talk to her if her mood toward him had thawed. They hadn't spoken much since he'd been removed from the construction detail. Though she was, Mattis noticed, quite chatty with Ingo, who seemed to visit their cell more often than his position ought to allow, as far as Mattis was concerned.

He was lost in this disheartening thought when, again, he stubbed his toe on a piece of debris.

"Ow!"

"What now?" Patch gave Mattis a shove to keep him walking, but Mattis stopped.

"Watch where you're going, Mattis," Jo demanded.

Mattis again examined the ground for whatever had tripped him. This time he saw it: a dingy metal cylinder about the size of his forearm. He didn't know how he'd missed it earlier, and he was surprised that none of the others had seen it, either. It was similar in size and shape to his weld-bar, and it struck Mattis immediately that it would make an excellent digging tool. He tried to casually toe some mud over it, but Jo watched him, so Mattis just lifted his foot and pretended to scratch his other leg with it. He smiled at Jo, who didn't smile back.

"Ready to go?" Jo asked—again, more a command than a question.

Mattis nodded. Ymmoss growled, then followed it with a louder bark and growl. Jo broke his study of Mattis to look over at the Gigoran, who carried on and on, probably complaining about the clumsy orphan from Durkteel. Mattis took the opportunity to kick mud and leaves over the metal rod he'd found. He'd need to remember this spot, so he could claim it later. He figured he had a few more circuits around the perimeter to try for his prize. Hopefully another distraction would present itself, and he could shove the tool into his pants or boot or otherwise hide it. He didn't have much optimism that this would happen, but there it was, like a ray of sunlight slicing through the heavy blanket of clouds: hope.

The third time around, Mattis had a moment of panic when he didn't see his treasure in the mud. He'd hidden it too well. He'd also been too distracted by despair and the sky to correctly remember the precise spot he'd left the tool. Fortunately, he tripped over it again.

"Ow!"

"Mattis!" Jo was fed up. "Get it in order, or I'll—or I'll—" Jo stopped, unable to think of a punishment worse than Mattis's current situation.

"Sorry," Mattis said softly, and resumed his walk. Jo had been watching Mattis as if Mattis were either a pressure bomb or about to dissolve into the mist. Mattis thought it was important to keep Jo calm, maybe even so relaxed that Jo would drop his guard and allow Mattis the opportunity to grab the debris. Mattis repeated, "Jo. Sorry."

Jo lowered his brow skeptically and nodded. "Just keep moving," he said.

Mattis noted the spot along the fence line as well as he could—a collection of brambles there, perhaps three hundred paces from the palace steps—and kept moving. Knowing that the object was there, waiting, made the trek around the perimeter interminable. His frustration skyrocketed when, just down the line, Mattis actually did discover a breach in the fencing that needed repair. It served him right, he thought, for actually paying attention instead of getting lost in a gloomy daydream.

He waited, a fidgety itch crawling up and down his limbs and between his shoulder blades. Ymmoss purred as she mended the fencing wire, either not caring or not revealing that she cared when the barbs stuck in her paw. While she did her slow work, Jo and Patch wondered what might have created the hole in the fence.

"It's a small tear," Patch said. "Maybe a paulef?"

"Paulefs have those delicate hands," Jo said. "This was bit clear through. A jhadd?"

"Strong. Talons. Razor-sharp beak. Coulda been."

Ymmoss growled.

"Does it matter?" Mattis translated, correctly or not.

Both Jo and Patch looked at Mattis. He shrugged and looked away. Next time, he wouldn't speak up.

Ymmoss finished her repairs, and all of them started again around the perimeter. This time, when they were nearing the spot where he'd hidden his find, Mattis was ready. He knew it was risky to further irritate his minders, but he didn't have a choice. As they approached the area—the collection of brambles, the mounded mud and leaves—Mattis threw himself into the muck face-first.

"Ooow!" he shouted, sliding and kicking about as if he'd tripped and was now stuck on something. He flung his weld-bar into the air and it landed sticking up out of the mud not far from him. He kicked around some more.

"Is it a dianoga?" Patch asked, flicking his blaster to life.

"No!" Mattis yelled. Then, more calmly, "No. I tripped. Got stuck on something."

But he didn't get up. He was just a meter from the metal rod. If he reached out, he'd be able to grasp it, but they would all see, and then it would be for nothing.

"Get up, Mattis," Jo sighed.

If he got up, he'd lose his chance. He stayed facedown in the mud. He blew a bubble of it from his nostril.

"Mattis."

Ymmoss roared. Alarmingly fast, as if she'd held all her energy in reserve until that moment, she yanked Mattis's weld-bar from the mud and wielded it like a sword. She took a hard whack at Patch, who caught the weapon in the chest, the blow cracking his armor. He was down instantly but just as quickly back on his feet. Patch reached for his FWMB-10 and aimed it at the Gigoran, but she was upon him, the muzzle of his blaster clutched in her grip. Patch fired and the plasma-blast went wild. Jo rushed to where they tussled over the weapon.

Mattis saw his chance. As fast as he could, he snatched the scrap. Another shot came from behind him and the mud around his head flew up. Just a stray shot from Patch's blaster.

"My shock-stick!" Patch shouted at Jo. "Get it! Get her off!"

Ymmoss was on top of Patch, clawing at his helmet and his armor.

Mattis yanked the metal rod closer to him

and hugged it against his body. He just needed to squirrel it away somewhere.

"Down your pants." Did that harsh whisper come from inside his own head? Was the Force done sleeping, finally? Mattis jolted from the voice and almost bumped skulls with Jo, who crouched over him. "Quickly. Hide that thing," Jo, not the Force, continued to whisper.

Was Jo really telling him to hide the tool he'd found? Mattis didn't dwell on the implications. He stuffed the rod into his belt and pulled his shirt down over it. The small lump it made was disguised by all the mud covering Mattis.

"Sir!" Patch yelled at Jo. Ymmoss roared, her face to the sky. Jo turned away from Mattis and reached down to snag Patch's shock-stick from his holster. He didn't wait for it to charge fully before zapping Ymmoss in the side with it. The Gigoran roared again and fell over into the muck, taking Patch with her. Mud flew. Ymmoss scrambled to a crouch, Jo zapped her again, and she again dropped into the mud. Patch recovered his blaster and regained his footing.

"Okay?" Jo asked.

"Fine," Patch reported.

"Prisoner!" Jo yelled at Ymmoss. She lay on her side in the mud. "Can you stand?" Ymmoss mewed, nodding, and got to her feet. "We're done here today. You have restraints, Ess-Bee-Three-Seventy-Nine?"

Patch did, and he tossed them to Jo.

"You're not going to give me any trouble, are you, prisoner?" Jo said as he approached Ymmoss. The Gigoran growled but shook her head. "That's good." Jo bound Ymmoss in the restraints and turned her back toward the palace. "She won't trouble you," he told Patch. "We're right behind."

Patch nudged Ymmoss with his blaster—clearly, he still didn't trust her—and escorted her to the detention center.

"You," Jo snapped at Mattis, who dropped his gaze guiltily. "Let's go."

Jo sidled up beside him and gave Mattis a sharp shove in the same direction. They were a few meters behind Patch and Ymmoss. Mattis thought he'd imagined Jo's unexpected cooperation earlier, but then Jo asked, very quietly, "You have it?"

Mattis nodded.

"Good. Get to work." Mattis nodded again. He opened his mouth to ask a question, but Jo cut him off. "Wanten believes I'm on his side. We need to coordinate on this—you, me, Lorica. We need to talk."

"When?" Mattis asked. "How?"

"*Shhh,*" Jo snapped. "I'll figure it out. Wanten has a desperate desire to get in good with the top brass of the First Order. I can string him along for a little while by telling him you and Lorica will break as soon as you're worn down. I've kept them from interrogating you this long. I'm hoping they let me do it. Are you listening to me?"

He was. They were getting closer to the palace steps, and Mattis was trying to remember what Jo was saying, word for word, so he could report it to Lorica accurately. But when that time came, he would only remember the most important part. He would only recall the last thing Jo said.

"I need you and Lorica to tell me everything you know about the Resistance. I'll put it together with what I know, mix it all up, and give Wanten a fake version. I need it to be believable, though, and that's why I need you two to tell me everything. Everything."

Before Mattis could ask any questions, before his brain could even process the information and conclude that perhaps the reason Jo wanted to know everything they knew was because he really *was* a traitor working for the First Order, they were back on the palace steps, where Patch was waiting.

"Bring both prisoners back to their cells," Jo told Patch. "And you," he added to Mattis. "Watch your step."

Mattis looked puzzled.

"Don't trip on these steps. You've made enough of a nuisance of yourself today."

It was something both the old Jo—Mattis's squad leader—and the new Jo—a young heir of the First Order—would say. Mattis ended his day more confused than ever.

CHAPTER
11

MATTIS WAS TOO EXCITED to get to work chipping away at the cell wall with his new tool to clean himself off much, so he was covered with uncomfortable drying mud and looking like something a rancor had coughed up when Ingo delivered Lorica back to their cell.

"That's a good look," Lorica told him as Ingo slid the cell door closed behind her.

"Go easy, prisoner," Ingo told Lorica. The way he said "prisoner" made it seem like just a bit of fun. Like he was calling her "pal" or "buddy." "Your friend has had a difficult day, from what I understand."

"That so?" Lorica asked. She had a playfulness

in her voice that shouldn't have been there after so many grueling hours working construction.

"I fell down a lot," Mattis said unhappily.

Both Lorica and Ingo laughed. It unnerved Mattis to see a First Order soldier happy. Lorica remained by the bars, keeping Ingo close. Maybe all that was happening was that Lorica's Zeltron abilities were affecting Ingo, but to Mattis, it seemed like more. He wished Ingo would go away. He wanted to tell Lorica about the tool he'd found.

Lorica was saying something about her day spent working on the wall, but Mattis couldn't hear her. The scratching in the walls had grown too loud. If he heard it, did that mean he was too far gone or that there was no coming back once he went crazy enough to hear it in the first place? Did it mean that his new hope, so recently acquired, was false? Didn't Lorica hear it?

"Don't you hear it?" he asked.

She stopped talking and looked at him as if he were insane, which was always possible.

"Sorry," he mumbled. "Tell me more about your wonderful day hauling timber and sheetrocking your own prison."

Lorica turned away from him and said something in hushed tones to Ingo.

Ingo looked around her to Mattis and said, "You'll be uncomfortable in those muddy clothes all day." Then he turned and left them alone.

"Mattis, what the *foito* are you doing?" Lorica flung a Zeltron swear at him.

"What am *I* doing?"

"Yes!"

"What am *I* doing?" Mattis repeated. He couldn't form a coherent thought, so insistent was the rasping sound from the wall behind his bunk. Whatever was in there, whatever was clamoring for his attention, was moving around, getting closer to him.

"Mattis, you don't seem well," Lorica said, sounding less angry. "You're covered in filth, you're sweating—"

"It's warm in here. On this planet."

"You're all flushed." She placed a few fingers on his forehead, and he jerked away. "I'm afraid you're sick, Mattis."

"I'm not *sick*," Mattis spat.

"You've been rolling around in the mud."

"I haven't—why won't it shut up?" He shook his

head, but the angry scraping wouldn't go away. He pressed his palms to his ears.

"Did you just tell me to shut up?" Lorica fumed.

Mattis couldn't hear her. He just shook his head, repeating softly, "No, no, no."

"Mattis, what is happening to you?"

"I found something," he said, as if he hadn't heard her. "I found something that could help." Mattis started digging in his bedding for the metal rod to show Lorica.

She grabbed his wrist hard to stop him. "Mattis," she said, locking eyes. "What's happening?"

The scratching in the walls or in his head or in his ears ebbed, and Mattis was able to focus on Lorica and only Lorica for a moment. "I found something that can help," he said.

"Help with what?"

"Escape."

"Mattis, I'm working on that. I talk to Ingo all day, every day. He's actually . . ." she trailed off, knowing, perhaps, that this wasn't something that Mattis wanted to hear but nonetheless finding it too important to let it go unsaid. "Ingo isn't a bad person."

"He's our jailer," Mattis scoffed.

She nodded. "Yes, but his involvement with the First Order is just . . . it's a matter of birth."

Mattis shook his head. He didn't understand or care to.

"He could be our way out. He's looking around at what's happening here and how Wanten is treating the prisoners, and he doesn't like it. He didn't realize what the First Order was really like. I think—Mattis, look at me." He did. She continued, "Mattis, I think I can convince him to join the Resistance. He's already open to it. He likes the things I tell him about what the Resistance is doing."

"He likes *you*," Mattis whined. "He's a First Order soldier, just like Jo, just like Aygee is now, and he doesn't care about the Resistance. He's falling in *love* with you."

They both let that sit there, unsure what else to say.

Then Lorica sighed, "He's not."

"Of course he is!" Mattis shouted. "Why wouldn't he be?" He wouldn't speak any further than that. He didn't like how much he'd said already. It felt too revealing somehow, too honest. Mattis turned away in his mind, and he ran down another avenue of thought. Something more aggressive and sulky. "You're probably falling in love with him, too!" Mattis shouted.

"Please stop yelling," Lorica said.

That only made Mattis angrier. He felt his face flush red and hot. He breathed in and out sharply through his nose like a tauntaun. "Tell me I'm wrong," he seethed.

"Of course you're wrong. We're just *talking*. He's listening to me tell him about the Resistance, and I'm listening to what he says about the First Order."

"Great." Mattis bristled. "Next thing, you'll probably get married, and then you'll be my new guard, since you love Ingo and the First Order so much."

"You're acting like a child."

"I'm fifteen!" Mattis yelled. "I'm not a child! I know things. I know how people are. I know how you are, because we used to be friends, remember?"

"We're still friends."

Mattis snorted, unable to come up with a response. He knew he was being childish, but he couldn't get his head straight between his exhaustion, his thirst, and the constant noise in the walls around him. Plus, the mud in his nose had dried. It felt gross.

"Mattis, I'm doing this to help us escape. If I have to join the First Order for us to escape, I'll do it."

Did she really just say that? Was Mattis now imagining conversations as well as the endless rasping? What had Cost called it? *Scritching-scratching*? Yes. That was what it was. Whatever was in there, it wanted to emerge into the world.

Mattis pressed himself against the wall and yanked his rough blanket up to his chin. He clenched his eyes closed so he wouldn't have to look at Lorica when he said, "Join the First Order then. Be with Ingo. I don't care. I don't care anymore. I don't care."

Lorica stared at him, disbelieving, not understanding. Something was happening to Mattis, and he couldn't explain it himself. From the look on Lorica's face, she couldn't help him or understand what was happening, either. He rocked rapidly back and forth, back and forth, whispering something under his breath. He was acting like Cost, but he was angry, too, unable to fully explain his feelings or thoughts, finding no difference between those two swarming storms spinning around in his head.

"I want to help you, Mattis," Lorica said. Her voice had a pillowy quality he'd never before heard from her. He wanted her to help him, so he nodded minutely. Lorica turned back to the cell door and called out, "Ingo!"

"No!" Mattis barked, then buried his head again in his blanket.

Lorica turned back toward the corridor and whisper-yelled for Ingo again.

"What is it?" Ingo asked. Lorica motioned with her head to Mattis on his bed, rocking and murmuring.

"Something's wrong with him," she said.

Ingo nodded. "Why don't you come with me," he said, punching on the cell's keypad.

"Should I leave him?" Lorica asked, worried.

Mattis was shaking now, pressing his head against the wall behind him. "You should leave him," Ingo said.

Mattis watched, mostly hidden under his lump of blankets, as Ingo took Lorica by the hand. Were they really holding hands while his brain melted in his skull? Would they skip through the hallways, laughing in a jolly way about how Mattis had no friends left?

Mattis heard Ingo say, "I'll put you and Cost in another cell tonight," as he slid the barred door closed again behind Lorica. "Let Mattis get his sleep. Let him think his thoughts in peace."

Mattis let out a hoarse, humorless laugh under his blanket. He wouldn't find any peace with his thoughts. The best he hoped for was sleep.

He didn't sleep, of course. Instead, he listened to the dogged scritching-scratching, losing himself in its urgency and the swirl of his own thoughts. Watching Lorica go away with Ingo felt like a dagger through his chest, and he had no way to extract it. Lorica was probably being fitted for a First Order officer's uniform already. She would do well there, with her adoration of rules (and Ingo) and bossing people around (and Ingo), and with her slippery moral center.

The thoughts and images were a tornado in his head, only touching down to do damage. He again saw himself growing old and remaining stranded there, in a detention center on a swamp planet. His old friends had turned into enemies—Jo and Lorica and AG—and only the reprogrammed droid, ageless, forever ticking, would remain to watch him turn gray and bent. Jo and Lorica would find their victories in the First Order. They were good soldiers and would make better officers.

He thought of Dec and Sari, lost in space, floating out there somewhere, dead. It was the deepest and most difficult concept for him to fathom; he swam around in its murky waters until the scratching took on a muted tone and then, finally, turned to laughter.

Mattis's eyes snapped open. The laughter ceased. The scratching was gone. There was silence in his cell. The gray day had faded to a darker night. Mattis wasn't shaking anymore, and he wasn't warm. He felt as if he'd sweated out toxins. He wiped the beaded perspiration from his face. He was alone.

Good.

He needed to be alone to do what he was going to do.

He'd hidden the scrap metal in Lorica's bunk. He remembered that now that his head was clear. He retrieved it and knocked it a couple of times against the bed frame to shake some of the dirt loose. Even in the growing dark, he was glad to be alone with the tool, and he could finally give it a closer look. It was a short, hollowed-out metal tube, probably used for shipping. It was locked, though; Mattis couldn't figure out how to open the chamber, but it might do to start busting through the cell wall. It was definitely sturdy enough to chip away at the already crumbling cement.

He figured a corner—the one where Cost had spent so much time—was a good place to begin. By chipping away there, he might create a hole where the cell walls met, but it was also easily concealed, should the guards arrive. He crouched down at the head of Lorica and Cost's bunk and started making small hits at the wall. The cement broke off more easily than he'd anticipated. It wasn't long before he had a mound of rubble and chalky dust around him. He looked around the cell for a way to cover it up. There was no drain in there; the bathrooms were down the corridor. He gathered some up in his cupped hands and deposited it in the bunk above his. He hoped they wouldn't be given another cellmate, for that prisoner would find his or her bedding filled with rocks and dust.

Mattis bent again to his work. Once he was through the first layer, the task became both more difficult and tedious. He tried not to think too much about how little progress he was making, how alone he was, how dark it was, and how desperate this work was. He stopped for a moment to clean out the dust that was accumulating in the tube.

The noise he'd been making continued.

Mattis looked at the tool then let his eyes roam the cell. How could the scratching continue when he'd stopped . . . ? Oh. He understood now. It was the scratching from before. The scratching that Cost had warned him about and that he'd heard when he lost all hope. But with this tool, hadn't he regained hope? Shouldn't the noise disappear?

Scritch–scratch–scritch.

It didn't disappear. And it wasn't just scratching. Now the laughter began again, too. High-pitched giggling and low-end chortling, echoing and trailing off so it sounded as if it were coming from all around him. Mattis put down his tool and dropped to his knees in the corner of the cell, as he'd seen Cost do so often before. The laughing continued. Unable to help himself, feeling the madness and despair and mistrust of what was real anymore erupting from deep within him,

Mattis laughed, too. At first it was just a bubbly, hesitant giggle, but that seemed to make the cell laugh even more, and as it grew louder, so, too, did Mattis, until he was bursting out with bellowing guffaws. He was crying, too, fat tears running down his face even as he howled with laughter.

What could Mattis do but laugh? And the walls laughed with him. So he laughed some more. And soon both he and the walls had a rollicking good time, laughing and crying, and Mattis was wondering when he would start hallucinating right about the time the cell door rattled open.

Okay, he thought. *Now, I guess. Now is when I start hallucinating.*

This wasn't any cheerful hallucination made of talking space candy or bantha balladeers; instead, Ingo appeared in the doorway. Backlit and foreboding, Ingo stared at Mattis, slumped against the wall. He nodded his head then walked away, leaving the cell door open. Was he allowing Mattis to escape? Was this more madness or could this really be happening?

Mattis rose, unblinking, not allowing himself to look away from the faint light of the open cell door. He was barely standing when a figure appeared in that light. At first he thought it was just his own shadow, but that was impossible. It was tall. It was hairy. It was Ymmoss.

The Gigoran stepped into his cell. She growled in a low, dangerous way he hadn't heard before. Without Lorica to protect him, Mattis knew he was doomed. Ymmoss would squash him beneath her enormous feet or rend him to pieces.

Mattis discovered that the metal rod was still in his hands. It occurred to him, as if the thought belonged to someone else, that this might be used as a weapon. It was sturdy and hard enough. Mattis was still confused from his bout of laughing and crying. Should he just hit her with the cylinder? That would be a good offensive strategy, his brain decided.

His thoughts were sluggish. They trudged through his mind like a Hutt playing offensive scooper in grav-ball. His pause stymied Ymmoss long enough that she stopped, too, to study him, and only when he raised the cylinder to strike her did she snap out of her own confusion and give him a sharp shove.

Mattis pitched back against the wall and his weapon slipped from his hand. He heard it clatter against the cement floor, and it disappeared into the darkness. The Gigoran approached him again. Mattis closed his eyes and waited for the fatal strike.

Instead of receiving it, he heard Ymmoss let out an abrupt noise somewhere between a whimper and a howl. He opened his eyes to find her bent at the waist and clutching the back of her head, mewling again with that pained noise. What had happened? Had Mattis finally unwittingly used the Force to battle his opponent?

From out of the dark a tiny figure leaped from Cost's bunk to Mattis's, swiping a glinting claw across Ymmoss's head as it flew through the air. Ymmoss yowled and thrashed at the air where the figure had been, but it was gone again. It disappeared into the shadows.

So, Mattis had failed to use the Force. Again. He did have some sort of savior in his cell, though, and for that he was grateful. While the Gigoran thrashed around, he took the opportunity to slide back into the dark corner in which he'd been digging his hole. A voice came from nearby: "Need more help, friend?"

Mattis, startled, leaped to his feet. Ymmoss

turned to him, fuming. She displayed her claws.

"Yes!" Mattis called. "Need more help, yes, now!"

He heard a familiar scratching, but this time he saw its source. The tiny figure squirrelled out of the narrow gap Mattis had made in the wall and sprung fearlessly at the Gigoran. It grasped her chest and slashed at her with shining claws. Ymmoss swung around and around, trying to free herself of her miniature shrouded assailant, succeeding only in pounding herself about the torso, yelping all the while.

The small figure dropped from the Gigoran's body and scurried under Lorica's bed. Ymmoss saw where it went and snatched the bunk, lifting it into the air and shaking it. The only items to come loose were blankets and pillows. Mattis pressed himself against the farthest wall, trying to make himself invisible. Ymmoss shook the bunk, but her attacker was gone. She smashed the bunk across the small room, and it went to pieces. The Gigoran, frustrated and injured, stalked out of the cell.

Mattis let out a throaty, thankful sigh. He looked around in the dark for his savior, but he couldn't see anything. Just shadows and the overturned, busted bunk bed. He pushed it against the wall where it had been, as well as he could, and returned to his own bunk. Dropping his head into his hands, he whispered, "Are you still here?"

He was answered with faint laughter. This time he didn't laugh in return.

"The door is open," Mattis said. "I could—*we* could just leave here."

But Mattis was paralyzed with fear. Ymmoss or Ingo or something worse might be right outside his cell, hidden from view, waiting to attack him.

The laughter rang out again, closer now.

"Don't you want to go?" Mattis asked. He'd feel better leaving if he had that tough little creature with him. Its claws had been enough to counter a Gigoran.

"Go where?" asked a voice that was equal parts broken glass and phlegm.

"Out. Away. Not here."

The creature revealed itself, crawling onto the foot of Mattis's bunk. It was rounder than Mattis had initially perceived, though it was still only as high as Mattis's thigh. It patted its stomach, squashing down the filthy wool that covered its

whole body. It had triangular ears that flopped around when it shook its head, and a pointed snout full of yellow teeth. The creature's mouth never seemed to close completely. It sat cross-legged opposite Mattis, as Cost had done only a few nights previous.

"Where to go?" the creature asked. "Run away? To get eaten by another of Mistress Harra's pets? Mistress Harra won't like Gherd getting et by the other pets. That's why Mistress Harra keeps Gherd in her lap."

"Are—are you Gherd?"

"Who else would be Gherd?" The creature laughed again. Outside of the echoing walls, his laugh wasn't so eerie.

"What are you?" Mattis asked. It was an indelicate question, but they were in coarse circumstances.

"Gherd is Gherd," Gherd replied.

Mattis shook his head. "No," he said. "I know you're Gherd."

"Gherd, yes."

"But what *are* you, Gherd?"

"Gherd still Gherd. What is Mattis?"

"You know my name?"

"And you know Gherd's!"

"Yes. No. I mean, how do you know my name?"

"Angry lady says it."

Mattis laughed, and Gherd copied him. "You mean Lorica," Mattis said.

"So angry," Gherd confirmed.

"You heard Lorica say my name, so you know my name."

"You heard Gherd say Gherd's name, so now you know Gherd's name." Gherd opened his muzzle in a panting smile. "Now you go."

"Go what?" Mattis asked. Gherd was infuriatingly confusing to talk to.

"Talk!" Gherd stood, his long arms hanging limply by his knobby knees.

"I was asking," Mattis began again, "what you are."

Gherd bopped himself in the head. "Gherd is still Gherd!"

"Okay, okay. Are you a rancor?"

Gherd's big eyes narrowed into slits. "What that means?"

"You aren't a rancor, are you?" Mattis said in the friendliest way he could. "And you're not a kinrath or a tawd, right?"

Gherd pulled his lips back over his teeth in revulsion. "Tawd dis*gus*ting," he snarled.

Mattis nodded in agreement. Tawds *were* disgusting. "Gherd isn't a tawd," he said. "So, what are you?"

"Gherd is—" The creature paused. Mattis could tell Gherd was about to repeat himself again, but then Gherd appeared to catch on. "Gherd is nanak!" he cried, and fell onto his back, laughing as if the entire frustrating exchange had been a long joke.

"What's a nanak?" Mattis asked.

"Gherd is!" Gherd lifted himself to his full meter height and brushed some of the filth off his woolly exterior.

"Of course. Gherd is. You're a nanak." Mattis understood what Gherd was conveying. "And you live here? In the walls?"

"Not always," Gherd admitted sadly. "Just now. Since the white-shells and the small Hutt Wanten come to Mistress Harra's palace."

Mattis began to put the story together. "You lived here with Harra the Hutt," he said, "whose palace this used to be."

"Mistress Harra is Gherd's mistress," Gherd agreed. "But the white-shells made holes in Mistress Harra's house. And small Hutt Wanten sent Mistress Harra away."

"Wanten didn't kill Harra?" Mattis had figured the First Order would have executed the
Hutt whose stronghold they'd invaded.

"No one can kill Mistress Harra!" Gherd
yelled. Mattis shushed him. The cell door
remained ajar, and Mattis didn't want Ingo or
AG or anyone else reminded of that until he'd
decided what to do about it.

"So Wanten just let her go?"

Gherd's head dropped and his ears drooped.
"White-shells were so, so mean," he said. "Dragged
Mistress Harra to the pod with other garbage-
beings. Sent her away to the stars in pod." Upset,
Gherd blew wet snot out of his snout, spraying
Mattis's blanket.

"What are the 'garbage-beings'?" Mattis asked,
wiping away Gherd's mucus with his sleeve.

Gherd shrugged his narrow shoulders, as if
Mattis should understand his odd descriptors.
"Garbage-beings are garbage-beings!"

"What do they look like?"

"All kinds. Little rounds and long shinies and
some like cylinders with wheels or spindles."

Mattis understood that Gherd was talking
about droids. The First Order must have evacuated Harra the Hutt's droids off-planet, along

with Harra herself. Gherd added, "Oh. Here's your cylinder. No wheels or spindles." Gherd reached behind him and pulled out Mattis's metal rod. Mattis took it from him and thanked him for finding it.

"Gherd finds everything. When Wanten the Hutt came with his white-shells and flew away Mistress Harra and the garbage-beings, they tried to make Gherd go away into the swamp with the other pets. But Gherd wouldn't go. Gherd belongs with Mistress Harra, and Mistress Harra will come home." As he recounted his story, Gherd seemed so small and alone. Mattis felt bad for the little creature. "Gherd hid in walls," he continued. "Plenty of room for Gherd. Can run, run, run around, too. Steal food from the white-shells. Don't steal food from Wanten, though. Hutt Wanten loves food like a Hutt!" Gherd slapped his leg and pealed into laughter.

"I'm happy I found you, Gherd," Mattis admitted. He was also relieved. The scratching in the walls, the laughter echoing through the cell, they weren't figments of his desperate imagination. He wasn't losing his mind. There was just a tiny woolly nanak living in the walls who was definitely, undoubtedly real.

"Gherd is happy you found Gherd, too," Gherd said. "Mattis was so alone, so sad." Mattis nodded. It was true. Gherd had been watching through the cracks in the walls, and he'd revealed himself to Mattis right when Mattis needed him most. "But Mattis won't leave Gherd, will you?"

Mattis had nearly forgotten the open cell door. Now might be his only chance to run. Gherd's question remained, however: to where? Even if he escaped from the detention center, he'd be out in the wild where there were rancors and tawds and other creatures that wanted him for breakfast.

Still, it was a chance. Maybe Mattis would do better facing a hungry menagerie than he would the First Order.

The thought was interrupted by the sound of footfalls in the corridor, growing louder. Someone was coming.

"Gherd," Mattis whispered. He was going to tell his new friend to hide, but Gherd was already gone. Mattis hadn't even seen it happen. The little nanak was quick and quiet when he wanted to be.

AG-90 appeared at the open cell door. "Talking to yourself again?" the droid sneered. "That road leads to planet crazy."

Seeing his old friend with his new programming made Mattis fume. He didn't respond. He
was afraid of what he might say.

AG didn't care, though. He just pulled the
bars closed and punched a code into the keypad,
and the lock slid true. AG strolled away, leaving
Mattis in his cell.

But this time, Mattis wasn't alone. He had
Gherd. And Gherd was going to help him escape.

CHAPTER

12

LORICA WAS ONLY a few cells away from Mattis, and she heard him yelling and muttering. She was worried about him. He wasn't the strongest of their little group (she considered herself to be) or the cleverest (also herself). She'd done what she could to help him in their time in the detention center, but she couldn't help feeling she'd failed him. Though she felt that he'd failed himself even worse. Still, she wished she could have done more. Mattis just made it so difficult sometimes. He didn't realize that the Zeltron people, due to their unique nature, experienced amplified versions of the feelings of those around them, especially those they cared about.

And against her better judgment, she cared about Mattis. His anxiety, his fear, and his general disquiet were all magnified in her when she was around him. But, then, so was his belief in his friends and in the general goodness of all people. And his sense of adventure. And his unwavering desire to help the galaxy. She was overwhelmed with affection when she was with him because he had affection for just about everyone. *Ugh.* Being a Zeltron was difficult. Experiencing emotions was difficult.

Now Lorica's emotions were a confusing mess. Thoughts got mixed up with feelings and all of them barreled around a track in her head like the podraces she'd watched back on Kergans, crisscrossing and bumping into one another so pieces broke off and memories flitted in and out of coherence. She was trying to get her head straight when Jo appeared at her cell door.

"Lorica," he said, jarring her out of her own jumble of thoughts.

"You coming in?" she asked. If she could get him to open the door, and if she could get him to step inside the cell, she knew she could fight him and win. Jo was strong and disciplined but, right now, Lorica might be stronger. Maybe she could entice him in the way she was working on mind-itching Ingo. She stood and approached the cell door. Jo just rested his hand on the bars.

"I'm not coming in," he said. He seemed unaffected by her. It made sense. Of any of them—including the droid—Jo was the least emotional.

"Then leave me to sleep."

"I'm going to get you out," Jo said seriously.

Lorica wasn't sure what to think. She'd argued with Mattis when he told her that Jo was a traitor to the Resistance. She'd spent more time with Jo than the others had; she felt she knew him, though, really, didn't she only know what he'd shown her? He was angry and militaristic. Those qualities served the Resistance expertly, but couldn't they equally well serve the First Order? Lorica lived inside others' emotions, although she was only just becoming aware how much. Surely she'd have known if Jo was lying to them, back on the Resistance base or on Vodran. And if he were a traitor and a spy, wouldn't he have just let them die in the sarlacc pit? She had trouble reconciling all the various versions of Jo Jerjerrod in her mind and in her memory: the leader, the hero, the suitor (and the suited, too), the spy, the traitor, the son of the First Order.

"I'll stay here, thanks," Lorica finally replied.

Jo began to speak, but Lorica stopped him with a sharp gesture.

"We don't need your help," she said. "We're doing just fine." She didn't tell him that both she and Mattis were working on their own escapes. She didn't trust him. She couldn't.

"Lor," Jo breathed. "I'm out here working for you."

"Yeah. Out there. You turned around awfully quickly, Jo."

"What good would I be if I were trapped in a cell with you and Mattis? Out here, pretending to be a First Order spy, I can keep Wanten and his soldiers away from you two. I can buy us some time while I figure out a way to spring you. And Mattis. And Aygee."

Lorica shook her head. It was true that she and Mattis had mostly been spared any attempts at information extraction by First Order soldiers, but Jo claiming credit for that was unprovable to her. More telling was his mention of AG. Jo had never liked the droid and must know that AG had been reprogrammed. Removing AG from Vodran as part of some vague escape plan would likely set off all kinds of alarms. And what would taking

AG with them accomplish anyway? He'd have to have his memory wiped and be reprogrammed again; he wouldn't be the droid that Dec called his brother anymore.

"Sorry," she told Jo. "We choose to stay."

From a few cells down, they heard Mattis fretting.

"He's not going to last very long," Jo said. It might have been the most honest thing Jo had told her. "He's losing it in there."

Lorica nodded.

"You have to believe me, Lor," Jo said. She didn't like when he shortened her name. Her mother used to do that. She hadn't liked it when her mother did it, either.

"I don't. I can't."

"What choice do you have?" The way he said it was brittle, and Jo realized it immediately. "I'm sorry," he said. "I'm sorry, really. But the circumstances are dire. I've kept Wanten distracted this long, but he's getting restless. He wants to impress the First Order. It's—it's a complicated story, but he has a long history with them and needs to make good. He thinks information from you and Mattis—more you than Mattis, to be honest—he thinks Mattis is kind of a dolt. . . ."

Lorica laughed at both Wanten's assessment of Mattis and Jo's old-fashioned slang.

"But he thinks you know something worth finding out, and he's not afraid to torture you to get it out of you."

"I can stand up to torture," Lorica responded, sounding tougher than she felt.

"Mattis can't. Wanten will go after him, too, just to get you to talk. I've told Wanten as many inconsequential things about the Resistance as I could. Like the kinds of droids they're using." Jo laughed dryly. "Wanten's attention drifts off when I start talking about droid specs, and he interrupts to ask about how he should redecorate the throne room. He really doesn't like to think about droids. So I try to talk about droids a lot. But pretty soon, he's going to demand more."

"Try talking about ships," Lorica suggested. "The First Order knows we fly X-wings, mostly, so just go on and on about them. Pretend you're Dec." She wasn't sure why Dec popped into her head at that moment—probably because he loved the tech of X-wings, and pretty much any mechanical thing, so much—but it made her miss him. They were often at odds back on the Resistance base, but they'd turned a corner on Vodran. She didn't think they'd ever be good friends, but Dec was a formidable sparring partner, both physically and verbally, and she liked that she never felt any dire affection or neediness from him, either. He just accepted her as another person, another foil, another squad mate. She was sorry he was dead. It hadn't struck her in any real way that he was until that moment.

If she accepted that Dec and Sari were dead, that AG was lost to her, that Mattis was losing his mind, then all she had left was Jo. Which meant she had to believe him, didn't she?

"What do you need from me?" she asked. She still didn't trust him, not completely, but she needed a contingency plan should Ingo get cold feet when the time came to release her.

"I need to know what you know," Jo said. "I've already told Wanten every insignificant detail I can think of. I need to be able to mislead him. Lorica . . ." Jo reached through the bars and touched his fingers to hers. "Do you know the location of the Resistance base?"

Lorica was not a stupid person. In fact, she was clever, crafty, and always noticed anything that might help her later on. She did know where the Resistance base was. She'd put it together shortly after they'd arrived, based upon the route of the shuttle that had collected the new recruits, the weather on the planet, and the flight patterns of some of the X-wing squadrons that had come and gone. The Resistance base was on D'Qar.

"The Resistance base is on Endor," Lorica told Jo.

Lorica wasn't stupid at all, which was why, though she had to trust Jo right then, she knew she could only trust him to an extent. She couldn't arm him with actual information with which to run back to Wanten.

"Endor?" Jo asked. "Isn't that a moon? The place with the—the little fellows."

"Ewoks."

"Why didn't we see any? Ewoks?"

"Because then you'd know we were on Endor. And the location of the base wasn't for us to know. I mean, you're the one who told me that."

"So how did you find out?"

"I went for a run one morning before training," Lorica lied. "And I ran right into an Ewok who was sneaking onto the tarmac. He—it—tried to eat me."

"Ewoks eat people?"

"I guess. I punched it right in its furry face,

though, and ran like a demon back to base." Lorica shrugged. "I don't know how General Leia brokered a peace with those little creeps, but that's the only encounter I know of with one of them. I guess she told them to leave us alone, and they did."

"Endor," Jo repeated thoughtfully, and Lorica nodded. "I'm going to tell Wanten a lie. I'm going to tell him the Resistance base is on . . ." He considered. "What's far enough from Endor but is realistic to have a base on?"

"Cole-Haddon?"

"It's inhospitable. No one would believe it."

Lorica tried again. "Hreeshi?"

"Hreeshi is nice, but as the home for a Resistance base? Maybe too nice. What about D'Qar?"

Lorica tensed. Was he onto her? Nothing in his face betrayed as much, but, again, Jo had always been difficult to read.

"What's the matter?" he asked. Apparently, Lorica was easier to read than Jo.

"Nothing." She tried to wave away his concern and project an air of innocence. "Do you think he'd believe it, though? D'Qar? Are there resources there?"

"I'm just picturing a map. And D'Qar makes sense."

Lorica nodded slowly, resigned to acceptance. Jo had settled on telling Wanten the Resistance base was on D'Qar, which was where it really was. It was possible he'd known this all along, but Lorica didn't know what to think anymore. Was Jo playing her? If so, he was certainly with the First Order. Or was he truly innocent and looking to deceive Wanten? If that was the case, then he might indeed be loyal to the Resistance. Lorica didn't know what to do.

The only thing she could think of was hastening her escape.

Jo touched her hand again and told her to remain optimistic. He'd feed the information to Wanten, hopefully distract the commander in that way, and then get Lorica and Mattis out of there. AG, too. Jo's face was lit up with what Lorica understood to be hope. She wished she felt it, too. Instead, all she felt was that swarming confusion as she turned back to her bunk. She listened to Jo's receding footfalls; they sounded like raindrops, and she stuck out her hand because, fleetingly, she thought maybe they *were* raindrops. She shook her head. Why was she so confused? Why was everything such a jumble?

"Are you confused, too?"

The voice came from within her cell. Lorica jumped back, slamming her shoulder blades against the upper bunk behind her. "Ow!" she cried.

Cost pulled the blanket off her head in the bunk opposite Lorica. She smiled, showing all her rows of teeth.

"Cost!" Lorica whispered. Lorica shook her head again, dispelling the cobwebs that had gathered there. Lorica must have magnified some of Cost's emotional turmoil.

"You saw your friend," Cost said. "But I didn't see him any."

"Jo, you mean? He might not be my friend."

"He's your friend," Cost affirmed. "He wants to help Lorica and Mattis. I want to help, too. Help Cost."

Help Cost. Her cellmate's plea was so simple. "We have plans in action," Lorica assured her. "When we get out of here—and we will get out of here—we'll bring you with us."

"You won't." Cost shook her head sadly.

"Cost." Lorica took the slim woman by her narrow shoulders and braced her, looking into her eyes. If she could make Ingo swoon and become malleable, then she could impart to Cost the truth of her statement. "We will. You'll come with us."

Cost nodded slowly, but she said, "I don't know."

"I do." Lorica let her go, and Cost disappeared again into the bedding. She was so slight that once the blanket was over her, she was gone. "Get some sleep. Rest your mind. Think of tomorrow."

"Tomorrow," Cost repeated. She fell asleep repeating it.

Tomorrow. Tomorrow. Tomorrow.

It was all Lorica could think of as she, too, fell into restless slumber.

When Wanten was handed his assignment on Vodran, he suspected it might drive him around the bend. He didn't think, however, that it would happen so soon. Since his arrival, not only hadn't he eaten a decent meal—his major indulgence and, for the past thirty years, his only pure happiness—but the walls had been talking to him. He feared, at first, that it was his imagination, but Wanten recognized that he didn't have a very good imagination and ruled out that possibility. He was left with the notion that there was something living in the walls of his new home. A creature, some remnant of that obscene Hutt, running about Wanten's throne room, Wanten's cells—even Wanten's dining room! The creature, whatever it was, might foul Wanten's food!

He tasked his personal guards with locating the creature. It took a fair bit of effort to convince them it existed, but after he made the guards sleep on the floor in his throne room (while Wanten slumbered in the quilted bedstead of the deposed Hutt), the guards agreed. There was something living there that Wanten hadn't brought with him.

His guards scoured the kitchen on the presumption that whatever was squatting in their palace was hungry. They made an ambitious mess, blasting a hole in the side of the kitchen, without much more success than a fleeting glimpse of the diminutive intruder, just enough to identify it. Its isosceles ears and gaping snout and, most of all, its woolly exterior classified their pest without question as a nanak from the planet Egips.

Wanten would have it destroyed. The interloper caused him to lose sleep. It mocked him from hidden places within his throne room, the throne room he'd stolen fairly from the Hutt. It told him he was worthless, that he'd squandered any potential he might have had under the Empire. It told him that the First Order didn't respect him and that they saw him as a crumbling relic of the former regime. The First Order pitied him.

It was possible that the nanak was just muttering an oddball salad of words and phrases, but it was what Wanten heard, and it angered him. As if his job weren't difficult enough! These stormtroopers were so by-the-book and not creative thinkers, not like in his day. They were eager, perhaps too eager. They too often fired first and didn't worry about the big picture, like plasmablasts wrecking his walls.

What's more, the facility he'd been tasked with turning into a detention center, Harra the Hutt's former palace, possessed a number of architectural problems. Most pressing and frequently addressed was the perimeter fence, which needed constant maintenance to barricade against the beasts that used to make the palace their home. Just the day before, one of Wanten's force—a keen stormtrooper with the call sign VC-2123, to whom Wanten had warmed—was gobbled up by a tawd. Wanten was sorry to see VC-2123 go. But the occurrence wasn't unusual. He lost stormtroopers too often to the hungry creatures in which the Hutt had trafficked. His facility also suffered frequent damage from that loosed menagerie. Luckily, Wanten had prisoners to rebuild the detention center. It kept them busy, which was another advantage, and if the prisoners were busy, they wouldn't notice what a meager crew Wanten had on Vodran. Wanten lived in constant fear of being overthrown by his prisoners, few of them as there were.

And then there was the arrival of the youths from the Resistance. Wanten disliked them. They made his stomach feel weak. They were such believers in their mission. It reminded him of himself, back in the old Empire days. He missed that young Wanten, though not enough to attempt to become him anew. He was too old, too tired, and had seen too much hypocrisy and bureaucracy. He knew too much about the way the galaxy worked. He wished to be rid of these young people. They exhausted him. Even the Jerjerrod boy, whose family Wanten knew and for whom he mustered a modicum of respect (leveled with a healthy dose of repulsion at the upper classes of the First Order officers), exhausted him. Jo Jerjerrod talked and talked—a lot about droids but also about spaceships and other things. Farming? Perhaps. After a certain point, Wanten's attention wandered, but he knew that, thus far, the boy hadn't told him anything useful. At least nothing that made him sit up straighter. When that happened, when Wanten's interest was piqued by some bit of information and his spine unfolded, he would know that he had something that would impress his superiors in the First Order. Wanten suspected that the Zeltron girl knew more than the Jerjerrod boy, but he wanted to give the boy a chance. After all, should it become public that he was dismissive of a son of the First Order, no information that he might offer would make a difference in his career.

"We have to catch that nanak," Wanten choked out to the stormtrooper nearest him.

"Sir?"

"I think that's our most critical issue right now, don't you?"

The stormtrooper wasn't one of his usual personal guards. "I don't know, sir," he said.

Wanten frowned, fleshy folds enveloping his lips. "I do," he told the guard. "What's your call sign, trooper?"

The stormtrooper turned to tell him but was interrupted by the appearance of Ingo Salik in the throne room.

"Commander Wanten," Salik hailed him as he entered.

Wanten didn't like his second-in-command. Wanten didn't really like anyone, but Salik was young, which was one good reason to dislike him, and physically fit, which was another. He was also well liked in the First Order hierarchy. Wanten wasn't sure why, then, Salik had been sent to Vodran with him—they'd told him something about "earning his stripes" and "doing the job of two men," Wanten vaguely recalled—but he really didn't care. Salik's confidence and matter-of-fact manner irritated Wanten.

"What do you want, Salik?" Wanten sighed. He looked around for something to occupy him—a beverage or some tassel on one of his pillows.

"A couple of things. The scouts we deployed a week ago have returned, sir." The way Salik said "sir" made Wanten's skin feel too loose.

"I thought they were dead."

"We lost two ships, that's true. But the pilot of the third ship is here now. Shall I show him in, sir?"

Wanten shifted. "Yes, yes, I don't know why you didn't just bring him in with you."

"I didn't know what you might be doing in here, sir."

Wanten looked at the stormtrooper he'd berated a moment ago, but the trooper just stared blankly back at him with those black lenses and shrugged.

"I was telling this waste of armor to catch that blasted nanak who's been causing so much trouble."

Salik already had his back turned and beckoned the pilot to enter. The pilot was a young man, too. Wanten despised him on sight.

"Tell Commander Wanten what happened, Humphris," Salik whispered. "But keep it brief. The commander has a tendency to . . . get distracted."

Wanten wished he hadn't flushed upon hearing his second's hushed warning, but it was nothing. His underlings respected him. That was why they felt they could joke around with him. He would make a special effort to pay attention throughout the pilot's report.

"What happened?" he asked.

The pilot, Humphris, carried a jacket over his arm. He handed it to Salik, who passed it to Wanten. "I chased the rogue shuttle through a debris field to this—there's a moon out there, sir. It doesn't get picked up on scans. I don't know why. It's populated by droids."

"Droids!" Wanten repeated in disgust.

"Yes, sir. They destroyed the rogue shuttle when I arrived and they told me that they tore its pilots to pieces. All that was left was that jacket."

"That happened a week ago!" Wanten said in realization. "Why didn't you return immediately?"

"The droids, they took me, sir." The pilot hung his head. "They locked me in a subbasement in their bunker. I was the only human there. They wanted to know if I was from the First Order."

"What did you tell them?"

"I told them nothing. Finally, after all of this time, I escaped. I knocked over an astromech droid and fled to my ship."

"Why didn't they destroy your ship as well?" Salik asked.

"They said it was good for parts that they could use to repair themselves. They said First Order ships are the best ships. I remember they said that several times."

Wanten nodded. That was true. First Order ships *were* the best ships. "A moon full of droids, eh?" Wanten said. "This bears consideration.

But, as long as they're up there, and we're down here, then we needn't worry about them."

"Sir—" Salik made to argue, but Wanten held up a meaty hand.

"I don't wish to engage droids, Salik," he said. "Besides, our pilot here says we won't find that moon anyway. I don't have the manpower to send a bunch of shuttles up there searching, do I?"

Salik agreed he did not.

"Thank you, um, pilot," Wanten said, unable to remember the pilot's name. "That will be all. Salik, was there something else?"

"Yes, sir," Salik answered through a set jaw. He waited for the pilot to leave before he continued. "The Genhu prisoner wants to speak with you."

Wanten pretended to distract himself by scratching his neck, which was sweaty, and then looking around for somewhere to wipe the sweat before deciding upon the pillow with the pretty tassels. In truth, he was trying to remember who the Genhu prisoner was.

"Bring the prisoner in," he said.

"She's nervous," Salik told him.

"She needn't be! I'm so nice! I'm really so, so nice." Wanten opened his arms wide in an effort to appear welcoming, but it made him tired, so he dropped them again.

His second-in-command turned and ushered in the rail-thin Genhu prisoner. Wanten remembered her now. She was his informant; it was the Genhu prisoner's job to tell Wanten what the other prisoners were plotting. It was so much easier than Wanten torturing them himself.

"What have you learned, prisoner?" Wanten asked. He was confident that there was syrup in his voice. He didn't like the way Salik blinked one eye when Wanten spoke, as if he were looking at a bright sun.

The Genhu prisoner's wide mouth moved, but Wanten couldn't make out her words. Before he could signal Salik to move her closer, his second-in-command scuttled her forward.

"Speak up, prisoner," Wanten said imperiously, but also, he hoped, generously. She should think she would be rewarded for betraying her fellow captives. She wouldn't, but she should think she would. That was Wanten's clever secret to maintaining tranquility in his detention center: to make promises he had no intention of keeping.

———

The informant stood before the commander of the detention center and bit her lower lip. Her mind had a habit of drifting away. Her teeth tapered into sharp points, and the tiny pain she felt from jabbing her own lip always brought her back to the present. She'd been confused since they'd arrived, the First Order and their piggy commander, and they took advantage of her confusion. They promised her more rations and more blankets if she would tell them what the other prisoners were saying and doing.

Cost told them, but she couldn't remember if she ever received those prizes. Her thoughts were a hurricane of confused activity, and they took advantage of that. The idea was fleeting; soon it was gone.

"We have a blanket waiting for you in your cell," Wanten told her. He grimaced in a way that Cost thought was supposed to make her calm. Instead, it made her queasy. Because Wanten looked queasy.

"Jo Jerjerrod doesn't like you," she said.

"That's not valuable information," Wanten said to Ingo Salik, who sometimes took care of Cost. Ingo talked a lot with Cost's cellmate, Lorica. Cost wondered if she should tell the piggy commander about that talk-talk-talking. Cost liked Lorica, though, and if she told the commander about the talking, maybe Lorica would get in trouble. Lorica had told something to Cost, though. Something that made Cost feel warm and thankful. What was it? If she could remember, Cost would tell the First Order people.

"Tell the commander something valuable," Ingo ordered Cost. His voice wasn't like a heated towel the way it was when he talked with Lorica. It was like rocks.

"Jo Jerjerrod likes the Resistance," Cost said. "He's going to free his friends." Cost swallowed hard as the ideas in her head closed into a point that she could read and recognize: she'd made a mistake. There was no taking it back. She'd doomed her new friends, the people who said they'd take care of her. She'd tried to tell Lorica that Cost would only help herself, that the First Order manipulated her, but the words had come out a jumble and Lorica hadn't understood. So now Cost did the only thing she could think to do: she kept talking. "After they escape," she said, "they're going to return and explode this place."

CHAPTER
13

THE NEXT MORNING, while Mattis was on perimeter detail, the bed Ymmoss had destroyed was replaced. When he returned to his cell, it was as it had been the week before. There was no evidence of a struggle. Mattis thought he'd imagined the nighttime visits from Ymmoss and then Gherd. His tether to reality was fraying, he knew, so he clung to what was real: the cell, the pipe with which he continued to chip away at the corner of the cell, and the outside world. If he hadn't seen the outside world daily during his work detail, he might have thought he'd imagined that as well.

In addition to the repaired bunk, Lorica and Cost were waiting for him in the cell. Mattis had pushed his own bunk against the growing hole he'd chipped in the wall. It was well concealed, as the corners of the cell fell in shadow naturally. Cost huddled on Mattis's bunk, above her usual corner where the hole was. The hole wasn't big enough for him to fit through, but in a couple of weeks it would be. Mattis was giddy with the anticipation of it. He couldn't wait to show Lorica and Cost, and he was about to do so when the cell door clanged open.

AG stood beside Ingo, both ramrod straight. Ingo's mouth was a thin, disappointed line. AG flickered his lens-lights a couple of times.

"This detention center has a security breach," Ingo told them. Lorica started toward him, but he stopped her with an upheld palm.

"Remain where you are, prisoner," AG said.

"We're here to excavate the wretch," Ingo said.

"Aw, if I'd known you were coming over, I'd have baked a pie." Lorica batted her eyelashes sarcastically. "But of course I don't have any flour or eggs or fruit or a cooker or, you know, anything except walls and metal bunks. So, sorry. No pie for you. Or me. Or anyone."

"We're looking for a nanak," AG announced. Mattis sensed Lorica relax. He wondered why she'd been tense. If Ingo and AG were looking for Gherd, surely they'd scour the cell and discover his escape hole. Lorica knew he was working on it, so why wasn't she nervous about them finding it? Or had she been worried about some other secret she held? There was too much to keep track of, Mattis thought. There were too many secrets.

"What's a nanak?" Mattis asked with pretend innocence.

"Never mind, prisoner." AG scowled. He pushed past them and moved into the cell. "Did some redecorating, huh?" He motioned to the bunks pushed against the wall.

"The ceiling dripped," Mattis lied, pleased that he'd thought of a good excuse.

"All the ceilings drip," AG retorted. He passed Mattis and pushed him gently down into Lorica's bunk. "Sit," he said.

"Ingo," Lorica began, "we're not harboring some creature. I think you know me better than that."

Ingo smiled despite himself. "You'd never have stood for that on Kergans. Mother would have called the exterminators immediately."

Lorica nodded and smiled. Mattis felt a pang of jealousy. He clung to his hope that AG and Ingo wouldn't find his escape hole.

"It comes here sometimes," Cost told AG as he roused her from her corner. She slapped her hand over her mouth and issued a muffled "Sorry."

"You've seen it?" AG asked them. "The nanak?"

Ingo told Lorica, "It's stealing food and other stuff. It's making Wanten crazy."

"Wanten's already crazy," Mattis said, then covered his mouth, too.

Ingo pretended not to have heard. "Wanten wants to have it stuffed and mounted on a wall. Hopefully in his new chamber somewhere. He thinks he'll be promoted to the Bittelari Cluster."

Static that sounded like a laugh came from AG's vocabulator. Mattis thought this odd for a First Order droid. They didn't find anything funny.

"Look around," Ingo told AG. He ushered Lorica off to one side of the cell and they spoke softly; Mattis couldn't make out what they said, but they gave off a sense of intimacy. Another stab of jealousy shot through him.

He took hope, though, in the fact that Gherd was not only real but was proving himself to be a thorn in the side of Wanten and his command. AG walked along the walls, tapping them, finding nothing, though what he expected to find by doing that Mattis wasn't sure. There wasn't any scratching in the walls or laughing from any dark hole. Gherd wasn't there, and that gave Mattis even more optimism. Gherd could come and go.

"There are tunnels under this facility," AG said, looking at Mattis, as if he'd read his thoughts. "Not big enough for a hunk like you, prisoner, so don't get any ideas, but big enough for a starving nanak."

"So he could be anywhere," Mattis said.

"He?" Ingo turned from his hushed conversation with Lorica to Mattis. "You know our nanak, Banz?"

"Not personally." Mattis shrunk back into the bunk. "I just assumed . . ."

"What did I tell you about that stuff, Mattis?" Lorica jumped in, saving him yet again. She touched Ingo's shoulder lightly; perhaps he didn't even notice, but his attention was suddenly back on her. "Mattis is lonely because we're spending so much time together," she told Ingo. "He imagines he sees friends, and his imagination is limited. Very, very limited. Like, his imagination could fit into a Jawa's thumbnail. Do Jawas have thumbnails? Do they have thumbs? I guess it doesn't matter, but you see what I'm getting at." She smiled brightly and spoke in a soothing, even voice. It didn't matter what she was saying. She was lulling Ingo back into an emotional trance.

It felt to Mattis as if they'd been talking for ages. As often happened when he was in Lorica's presence, time took on a hazy, floating feeling. Whatever she was doing now permeated the room so that Mattis felt at once sleepy and calm. Even Cost was sitting quietly now in her same spot. Mattis felt a vague sense of surprise that AG hadn't moved her so he could look behind the bed, but neither could he be troubled with any anxiety at all.

AG-90 was the only one unaffected, which was to be expected, since he was a droid. He continued his search of the cell. It didn't take long, of course, but AG appeared to make a thorough investigation of the upper corners and walls. At least inasmuch as Mattis's clouded perception allowed him to see.

"There's nothing here," AG finally proclaimed, bringing them all back to dank, cold reality.

"As we expected," Ingo remarked. "I'll let you tell Wanten."

"Tell me what, Salik?" Wanten was there, his mass filling the open cell door, his hands held behind his back.

"Sir!" Ingo shouted, surprised.

"Yes, Salik. I'm here. Hi. Hi, everybody. Prisoners."

Mattis and Lorica both suddenly found the floor an appealing place to study.

"I understand that you don't want to say hello to me. That's okay. You're impolite. If you were polite, you'd be in my position. If you were polite, like Salik here, like your reprogrammed friend here, you'd work for the First Order and make something of yourselves."

Wanten didn't enter the cell. Mattis was glad. It was crowded in there already, and Mattis had once before been in close quarters with their captor. The acrid smell of sweat was overwhelming.

"You know who didn't make something of himself?" Wanten asked, trying to catch first Mattis's then Lorica's eyes. When he couldn't,

Wanten found another way to get their attention. He threw Dec's jacket onto the floor, where it landed with a flat whack.

"Your friend," Wanten said. "Your friend turned out to be nothing."

"We knew he was dead," Mattis said through a clenched jaw.

Wanten smiled. His teeth were big and blocky. "Yes, but before, I wasn't sure. I had your droid here"—Wanten said *droid* as if it tasted bad—"tell you that simply to break your spirit. Did it work? It worked, right?"

Mattis's and Lorica's eyes met, then both looked back to Dec's jacket on the floor.

"It was a good plan. I have so many good plans. Your droid told you your friend is dead; you got sad; you stopped thinking about escaping." He grinned. "But then, ah-ha! I find out that your friend really *is* dead! Up on some moon. I don't know. I wasn't listening, but he's definitely dead. My pilot saw it happen."

Wanten folded his hands in front of him. He was so calm. "So, I had a good plan, it turned out to be a good plan. So all of my plans are good plans. Want to hear another good plan?"

Neither Mattis nor Lorica reacted. AG said, "I do."

"Bring in our new prisoner!" Wanten shouted. A stormtrooper—Patch, Mattis realized, once he came into view—brought in a broken, bloody prisoner whom Mattis didn't at first recognize.

"Jo!" Lorica shouted. Mattis could see that she wanted to rush to Jo, to pick him up from where Patch had deposited him on the cell floor, but if she did so, her spell over Ingo would disappear.

Wanting to help her, Mattis shouted, "Don't get upset, Lorica!"

Taking his hint, she threw her face skyward in anguish. She fell forward and let Ingo catch her. He held her up. Mattis, happy they'd communicated and were apparently on the same page, knelt down beside Jo. He knew this would relieve Lorica's worries about him, that Jo might open his eyes to see a friend.

"You want to know what happened?" Wanten gloated.

"No," Lorica seethed.

"Don't listen to him," Jo managed to utter. "He lies."

"I lie?" Wanten was offended. "The hypocrisy

in here is as thick as the humidity! I lie? You lie. You lie, Jerjerrod. You told me you were a friend of the First Order. A loyal servant. But you're no friend. You're no spy. You're a Resistance loyalist through and through. You were going to help your friends here escape! Did you think I wouldn't find out?" Wanten was yelling now. No one respected him. He pounded a wall. "This is my detention center! This is my palace! I know everything that happens here!"

They all stood in stunned silence while Wanten panted after his brief tantrum. He folded his hands over his belly again. "What's going to happen," he said, "is this. This boy will be sent to the First Order, where his parents and their commanders can decide what to do with him. I bet they'll torture him. I would. But I don't have to. I have you two." He motioned to Mattis and Lorica. "I'm going to find out if you two know anything more of use. I'll probably have an old friend torture you. That would be ironic, wouldn't it? I bet you don't know anything, but I'll have your droid torture you anyway."

He jerked his head for AG and Ingo to join him outside the cell. They did, and Wanten slammed the door closed. Wanten pushed his face against the bars, as if they wouldn't be able to hear him if he didn't. "Sending this kid to his parents? Torturing the two of you? They'll promote me for sure. I'm going to be a hero of the First Order, as I was meant to be," Wanten gloated. He clapped his hands. "So thanks for all of your help. I could not have accomplished any of this without you."

As Wanten left down the corridor, flanked by Ingo and AG, Mattis heard him say, "Did you find that nanak? No? We should do that still, I think. Just check everything off . . ."

Mattis helped Jo onto his bunk. Jo reached up and grabbed Mattis's shoulder.

"I'm sorry," he choked.

"You didn't do anything," Mattis assured him. "You were helping us." He had been the whole time. Mattis should have trusted him. Jo had even helped Mattis smuggle that metal rod inside, and still Mattis hadn't fully realized that Jo was working with them, for them. "I'm sorry," he told Jo.

Jo shook his head weakly. "About Dec," he said. "*I'm* sorry."

Mattis felt the world slip away from him. Darkness seeped in at the edges of his vision. Dec was dead. He was really dead. It was like his friend had died all over again, only this time there was no room for doubt. Dec was dead.

Mattis repeated it over and over in his mind. It was all he could do. It made it at once real and unreal. Dec was dead. Dec was dead. Dec was dead.

Dec was dead.

CHAPTER

14

DEC WAS ALIVE. He wasn't sure for how much longer, but for the moment, he was alive.

He didn't know how long he and Sari had been guests of the droids; it could have been days or weeks. It felt like a lifetime. They were still in their filthy clothes, as droids weren't terribly interested in hygiene. They'd been fed, though not much and not well. Sari was listless with hunger. Droids didn't care about food, either.

They did seem to care about Dec and Sari. J-9A, the navigation droid who was apparently the leader, called Dec and Sari her guests. Sari had remarked, later, that J-9A gave it a sinister undertone, but Dec wasn't sure. Yes, there was something abnormal about the droids. Partly, it was their pack behavior. Each droid had a distinct, somewhat broken-down personality, but they were united in purpose. As yet, Dec was unsure what that purpose was. Sari maintained that, though the nav droid was the leader, she and Dec were prisoners being held until the scary medical droids could experiment on them.

"Why would a droid experiment on a human?" Dec reasoned.

"I don't know!" Sari cried. "Maybe they've already dismantled and rebuilt themselves and they're looking for something new!"

That had been on what was probably the third day. They hadn't been dismantled yet, so Dec considered them safe from that threat. The question remained: What did these droids want with them?

Earlier, J-9A had come into the small chamber in which they were being kept to let them know that the menace of the First Order was no longer upon them.

"What does that mean?" Dec asked.

J-9A took a weird sideways skittering step,

something he noticed she did when challenged. These droids were broken.

"It means you are safe again," she replied.

"Did you . . . kill them?" Dec asked.

"Did you take them apart to see how they tick?" Sari muttered.

Another sideways skitter. "People do not tick. People are filled with squishy bits and delicate meat chunks. We know how people work," J-9A replied. She lifted then lowered her pneumatic shoulders in an odd shrug. "We possess a great deal of knowledge." She cocked her head at Sari and her servos whirred. "Do you really think we'd need to dismantle a human to understand one?" J-9A laughed, a digital buzzing sound. "We have generations of knowledge in our permanent drives! We can access information about billions of subjects—"

An astromech beeped and booped atonally, interrupting J-9A. She responded, "I know they're not interested. I am simply tired of being underestimated." She moved to the door to leave with the astromech, saying, "Take a person apart, indeed. We allowed the shuttle pilot to escape back to Vodran. He believes you to be dead and will report as much to his commander. So, you see, you have nothing more to fear." Before sliding closed the chamber door, she added, "From the First Order."

Since that meeting, Dec and Sari had talked themselves weary trying to figure out what J-9A might have meant. Should they fear their captors? And if so, why had the droids helped them by getting the First Order off their tails? Or was there something else they should be afraid of, something even worse from which the droids were protecting them? The idea of that being true kept them from attempting an escape.

But maybe they were wrong. Either way, Dec reasoned, enough was enough. It was time to go.

"Sari, girl, we gotta get outta here." Dec nudged her awake, and Sari pushed him away.

"I'm staying. I like droids." She was just being difficult.

"Sari, even if there's something out there, at least it's *out there*. We can't stay in here forever."

"We don't have a ship!" She lifted herself to a sitting position. "We're stuck on this moon, which, to remind you, no one knows exists. So, I don't see how getting out of here would make much difference, do you? We'd still be stuck."

"Maybe I just want some fresh air," Dec replied. "Think you can open this door?"

"Of course I can," Sari scoffed. "I just don't want to."

"Sari, I'm serious."

"You're Dec Hansen. You're never serious."

"This time I am. There's half a chance our friends are still alive down on that planet. Which means we gotta go get 'em."

Sari shook her head. "I know," she sighed. She managed to get to her feet. The lack of food and exercise had taken a greater toll on Sari than it had on Dec, and he worried for her. All the more reason to get out now.

Sari crossed the small chamber to the door. She was a hacking whiz. She'd hacked security doors all over the Resistance base for many of Dec's mischievous pranks. The ramshackle security arrangement in this bunker shouldn't present a challenge to Sari and her incredible skills. She searched the edge of the security door for a weak spot, found one, then dug her fingers underneath a wall panel and yanked it loose, exposing the wires and circuit board beneath. "Do you have any tools?" she asked.

"Why would I have tools?"

"Did you think I was just going to get this door opened with my mind?"

"I didn't think about it," Dec admitted.

She tossed the wall panel onto the floor then slumped down beside it. "Dec," she grumbled.

"I thought you always had that kinda stuff on you!" he pleaded. "You're like this super hacker person. All brains and know-how!"

"Yep," Sari agreed. "But I'm not a sorcerer."

Dec crossed his arms and stared at the security door. Finally, he said, "Okay," as if he'd cracked the problem.

"What?"

"We do it the hard way."

"What's the—"

Before she could complete the question, Dec was jogging the short distance to the door and slamming himself into it. Hard. The wind knocked out of him, and he let out a loud "Oooomph!" Then he turned, walked back to where he'd been, and did it again. *Smack!* "Ooomph!"

"Dec," Sari began.

He threw himself into the door again. It didn't budge.

"Dec," she repeated. He was going to knock himself unconscious if he wasn't careful.

Smack! "Ooomph!"

"Dec!" she finally shouted. He held up a finger, panted a few times, and then again threw himself at the door. *Smack!* "Oomph!" Nothing.

Sari stood again, reached out a long arm, and held Dec back as he readied for another run. Anchoring him in place, she stepped forward and gave the door a mighty kick. Sari was big and strong and, while she didn't always like to use her strength, she'd do pretty much anything for her friends, especially Dec. The door fell outward with a thunderous slam, and all of a sudden their freedom was before them.

"Thank you," Dec said.

"You're welcome."

"Let's go."

"Go where?" Sari asked, peering into the dark beyond the door.

"I reckon we'll find out."

CHAPTER

15

THEY SAT BY JO, tending to his wounds and nursing him back to something resembling good health. He was beaten up, but worse, his spirit was broken.

"We're not going to let them take you to your parents," Mattis told Jo.

Jo shook his head weakly. "You are. You can't risk your own lives."

"We can and we will." That was Lorica, more resolute than Mattis had ever seen her. And he'd seen her *really* obstinate. "When Ingo returns, I'm going to make him open this cell and let us out. Maybe he'll even come with us."

"And if that fails, I have this hole," Mattis said, leaving Jo's side and dragging the bunk away from his barely dug tunnel.

"That's a great hole, Mattis," Jo said sarcastically. He winced with pain as he laughed.

"Hey! Don't make fun of my hole." Mattis was feeling very sensitive about his efforts. After all, his escape plan was going better than Jo's, wasn't it? Jo had been found out by the First Order, whereas no one yet knew about Mattis's tunnel.

Lorica and Jo laughed at him some more. "Mattis," Lorica said, "you've barely made any progress. Let me work on Ingo some more. I'm sure I can push him to free us before they come for Jo."

Jo pushed himself up so he was leaning against the wall. "Forget your hole for a minute," he told Mattis.

"I'll never forget my hole. Someday that hole is going to be a tunnel."

Jo shook his head in good humor. "Just for a minute."

"Fine. But I don't want to talk about Lorica using her woo-woo powers on Ingo anymore."

"Are you threatened because my plan is going

to work and your hole isn't big enough for a space beetle?" Lorica scoffed.

"Forget Ingo, too," Jo said.

"Huh?" Both Lorica and Mattis shot Jo questioning looks.

"Just—just for a minute," Jo clarified. He sighed and offered them a pained smile. Smiling was unusual for Jo. It was even more unusual considering their circumstances. "I'm about to be punished by the First Order," he reminded them.

"We know. That's why we're talking about getting you out of here," Lorica countered. Then, to Mattis, she added, "I think he might have brain damage."

"My brain is doing great," Jo told her. "I just want to talk to you two."

"We're talking," Mattis said. "These are words. I'm saying them. Words, words, words."

Jo laughed dryly. "This is what I want," he said. "I'm about to leave you guys forever. I don't know what the First Order will do to me. I don't think they'll kill me; my parents aren't that heartless. But I'll never return to the Resistance."

"Jo . . ." Mattis started to tell Jo that he was being silly. Surely he would return to them.

But he couldn't be his usual optimistic self. Not now. Jo was right. Once Wanten sent him away, Jo would be gone forever. Mattis was surprised to find himself depressed about this. He and Jo hadn't gotten along very often, but after everything that had happened on Vodran, and the way Jo had stuck his neck out for them, he realized that they were friends after all.

Jo nodded, as if he'd read Mattis's mind and was confirming their friendship. "I just want to remember something good," he said.

"I want stories, too!" Cost chirped from her place in the bunk above Lorica. Mattis had almost forgotten she was there.

"Did anything good actually happen back on the base?" Lorica said snarkily.

"I met you guys," Mattis said. It just fell out of his mouth.

"You mean, you met Dec and Aygee," Lorica said.

"No," Jo corrected her. "He means us. Right, Mattis?"

"Yeah," Mattis admitted. "I mean, I know we weren't friends at first, but I looked up to you two. Even though you were *so mean*, Jo."

"I wanted to make you a good pilot."

"I know. You just didn't count on having a bunch of recruits who didn't follow the rules that you understood. Me, Dec, Aygee-Ninety, Klimo. The way you learned to train us isn't the way we're built to learn, I guess. I'm sorry about it."

"You're going to be a great pilot," Jo told him sincerely.

"I hope I am," Mattis replied. "And if I am, it's partly because of both of you. You weren't always so bad."

"We weren't? Darn. We tried to be," Jo joked.

"What about Snap and Karé's wedding?"

"There was no wedding between Snap Wexley and Karé Kun," Jo said seriously, and they all laughed. Because, of course, there had been. It was the worst-kept secret on the Resistance base. Somehow, J-Squadron had wound up right in the middle of it.

Snap Wexley, Karé Kun, and the rest of Black Squadron were all idolized by the new recruits. They, under the command of Poe Dameron, got to go on all the cool missions. And they, under the orders of Poe Dameron, were tasked with carrying out the secret wedding. Like everything

J-Squadron had a hand in, though, it had been a disaster. Fortunately, Snap and Karé's wedding was a *hilarious* disaster.

Poe had instructed Jo that the Resistance leaders should not find out about the wedding; General Leia and Admiral Ackbar and the others already had enough on their plates without worrying about the love story between a couple of their best pilots. He asked Jo if J-Squadron could help. So Jo gathered J-Squadron and dictated to each of them their duties for the secret wedding. Naturally, Jo didn't consider anyone's strengths or interests before handing out orders. He simply had a list of what had to be accomplished and tasked his recruits with each item.

That was how AG-90 wound up in charge of music, which turned out to be a happy accident. AG did a bit of fiddling with his vocoder and was able to turn his usually tuneless warbling into a sweet, melodic quaver that trilled like some pastoral bird or a relative of an axton-tarsier, those big-eyed, floppy-eared furry pets native to Ques. It was a lovely, if unrecognizable, tune to accompany Karé down the makeshift aisle that Sari had created. Sari outdid herself, scrounging for materials and then foraging in the nearby woods for decorative flowers and branches and the like. She transformed the little corner of the tarmac where the ceremony was held into a woodland hideaway.

The trouble arose because of Mattis and Klimo's assignment. They were put in charge of food. That actually hadn't been one of Poe Dameron's requests—he reasoned, smartly, that it would be too difficult to prepare anything special on the base. They had access to what was in the mess, and that was all. But Jo, wanting to impress the older pilot, insisted. And because he didn't himself know what to do, he put Mattis and Klimo in charge of "preparing something special" for Snap, Karé, and their guests.

"They got something special, all right," Mattis said, remembering. "They're definitely not going to forget the food."

"Or what the food did to everyone," Jo agreed.

Mattis was handy in the kitchen. Growing up at the orphan farm on Durkteel, he'd learned to prepare foods with meager supplies for the younger kids. Oddy Muva of Black Squadron gained Mattis access to the mess hall, and Mattis and Klimo got to work. Mattis mixed up some crackling pudding from crackling pods and canned bantha milk. He wished he'd kept an eye on his concoction, though, because he later learned that, when he wasn't looking, Klimo took the opportunity to throw in a dash of anilam, the powdered flavoring harvested from izy-leaves. Mattis didn't know where Klimo found izy-leaves. Later, they were all laughing and farting too hard to figure it out.

As the host, Jo had the not-so-bright idea that all the attending wedding guests—which included almost everyone on the base, except for the leadership—should eat Mattis's pudding before the ceremony. Which meant that everyone was happy and full during the dewy-eyed procession and heartfelt vows.

Poe himself officiated the wedding of his friends. If he felt the same rumbling in his guts that everyone else did as the ceremony proceeded, he was too cool a customer to show it. But he must have, for when it came time for him to ask if Snap Wexley took Karé Kun to be his wife, he only got as far as, "Do you, Snap Wexley, take Karé Kun to be your—" before his insides erupted in the most atmosphere-ripping flatulence the galaxy ever heard. Everyone laughed, because they sympathized. Their insides were doing somersaults as well.

But Poe Dameron was always cool, and he began again, asking, "Do you, Snap Wexley, take Karé Kun to be your wife?" managing to get the whole sentence out that time.

Snap was not so lucky. "I—" he began, and what followed was a four-alarm fart that lasted longer than the ceremony itself had thus far.

A wave of laughter washed over the crowd. And then again when Karé, in disbelief, yelled at her soon-to-be husband and then let out a deep, meteoric toot herself. She slapped both hands over her face, completely embarrassed, as Snap, Poe, and everyone else just let laughter reign.

Because soon, everyone who'd eaten the crackling pudding was sounding off like firecrackers, tooting and honking and letting loose with all kinds of gassy exclamations. It was mortifying and uproarious all at once. Mattis stood beside Jo, who emitted a high-pitched *wheeeeeet!* that was unlike anything anyone had ever heard. After it happened, Jo glared at Mattis as if to say, *This is your fault.* His anger was undercut, however, by another flatulent bellow and then peals of laughter that he just couldn't help.

None of them could.

Amid the squeals of laughter and clamor of

gut-ripping gas, Snap and Karé were married, AG, Oddy, and some of the others struck up a happy musical beat, and everyone on the Resistance base laughed and danced and farted late into the night.

Jo didn't punish J-Squadron because, as he said, no one would ever mention the event again but in hushed whispers, but Mattis knew Jo had other reasons. It was because he'd had fun. It had been wild and silly, and there wasn't a lot of opportunity for that in the Resistance. Fighting against the forces of evil was serious business, as it should be, but sometimes it was helpful to let loose and laugh. Mattis suspected Jo knew that, and that was why he didn't exact any punishment.

"So, thanks," Mattis said now, in their cell on Vodran. And as if to punctuate his point, Mattis released a prolonged monotone fart.

"Oh, Mattis, come on!" Lorica yelled, waving her hand in front of her face.

"You know you had fun, too," Mattis scolded her. "Admit it. You like us."

"Leave me out of your love fest," Lorica said. For someone with a strong connection to emotions, she really tried to keep herself away from them.

"Lorica, you report for this love fest straight-away, soldier!" Jo ordered with a laugh.

"Not funny," she told him.

"I think someone needs a hug."

"I don't need a hug." Lorica scowled.

"You're getting a hug," Mattis said, and helped Jo to his feet.

The two of them wrapped themselves around her and, though she remained stiff and guarded, she laughed and said, "Okay, okay, I'll miss you when you get thrown in a First Order cell."

"I'm already in a First Order cell," Jo pointed out, releasing Lorica and returning to the bunk with no small amount of hurt.

"But maybe not for long," Mattis said. He was resolved, especially after that trip down memory lane, that Jo wouldn't be taken from them. "There's still the hole. If we work together, we can—"

"No!" Cost bolted upright in her upper bunk so forcefully she nearly hit her head on the ceiling. "Don't say it! Don't talk about it!"

"Cost," Lorica said in that calming way she had.

Cost put her hands over her ears and shook her head, as if she could resist Lorica's emotional sway. "No, no, no, no," she repeated. "Don't say it. The walls talk! The walls talk!"

"That's just Gherd," Mattis told Cost, lightly grabbing her wrist and pulling it from her head. "He's a friend. And he can help us, too. He knows the tunnels in here. He can dig out with us. All together, Cost."

"No, I am the ears of the wall!" Cost wailed.

Cost had crawled back into her confused mind, Mattis figured. He was worried about her, but she was just another plate on the buffet of worries he presently had. And he didn't have time to decipher her ramblings. He had to work on his tunnel, he had to protect Jo, and he had to make sure that Lorica wasn't slipping into true emotions for Ingo. His bounty of anxiety-inducing tasks was overflowing.

"She's been spying," Lorica said, as realization dawned on her.

"What? Cost? No." Mattis waved away the idea. How could Cost spy on them? She barely knew what was real. She had no memory; the thing with the tentacles had taken it from her.

"Yes," Lorica said, turning on Cost. "She was the only other one in the cell when Jo came to tell me he was working on an escape plan."

Cost's eyes were like two moons, pale and welling with liquid. She nodded limply. "I told," she sobbed.

Jo was halfway out of the bunk before the pain hit him and he had to stop. "You got me roughed up," he said angrily. "They could have killed me."

Cost sobbed some more.

"She didn't know," Mattis explained. He knew that was true. Cost would never have willfully sent any of them to harm. After the things she had told Mattis about her own travails, he couldn't imagine she'd ever try to hurt someone else.

"They talk and talk," Cost pleaded with Jo, trying to make him understand her. "Confused Cost."

"See?" Mattis said.

"Why are you defending her?" Jo barked.

"Jo, don't get upset," Lorica said calmly.

"I'm upset!"

"Stop yelling!" Cost covered her ears, trying to retreat from them.

"You doomed us." Jo pointed harshly at Cost. "You doomed us all. I could have gotten us out of here. All of us."

"Do you really think you're smarter than I am, Jerjerrod?" A new voice joined them from the other side of the bars. It was Ingo, drawn by their arguing. "Are everyone's secrets coming out to play? See, that's what we do. We make you fight each other, so you don't fight us. We give you secrets or we take them away. Isn't that right, Lorica? Do you want to tell the group the secrets we have?"

Lorica shook her head. The color had drained from her face. Mattis could see that she didn't want to tell her secret, whatever it was. And Mattis was certain, whatever it was, he didn't want to hear it.

CHAPTER

16

IT WAS DARK throughout the bunker, and Dec and Sari walked with their hands out in front of them, feeling their way along the wall, hoping they'd find another door and that door would lead to freedom. Groping their way through shadows wasn't Dec's idea of a fast or clean getaway, but he'd take it. Anything to get out of there.

They made turn after turn, but they seemed stuck in the black box of the bunker. Dec's outstretched fingers pressed against something damp and spongy.

"Is that you?" he asked Sari.

"Is what me?"

He squeezed the clammy, porous meat a couple of times. "That," he said. "Is that you?"

"Dec, I don't know what you're talking about."

A laugh came from the dark; Dec felt the flesh jiggle with the shallow chuckle. He snatched his hand away. "Who's there?"

An immense shape moved in front of them. It laughed again. Then, in a voice that was like hundreds of pebbles rolling downhill, it said, "You aren't droids. I don't think you're droids. Who are you?"

"Don't worry about us. We were just leaving." Dec recognized the shape of the creature in front of him. It was a Hutt. Dec did not want to spend more time than was necessary with a Hutt.

"No," said the Hutt. "I don't think you—hey!"

Suddenly, they were surrounded. The droids emerged from the shadows, their lenses and sensors lighting the area so that Dec could make out the purplish hue of the sweaty Hutt's skin and the way she stuck out her warty tongue in surprise.

Knowing the reputation of Hutts, Dec expected anger at the interruption. He expected violence of some sort, or at least a scolding. What he didn't expect was what happened. The Hutt backed away as the droids approached, lowering

her sluggish mass as well as she could, supplicating herself with a series of head-bobbing motions. Her thick tail swept the floor as if it were searching for something.

"You're out of your chamber," J-9A announced.

"We didn't—" Dec began to formulate an explanation that would be an elaborate if believable lie. But the nav droid had turned to the Hutt.

"Harra the Hutt," she said, "we've told you. It's dangerous outside of your chamber."

"I'm sorry, Jay-Nine-Ay," the Hutt responded. "You told me, and I'm sorry."

"You get lonely," J-9A said. Some of the droids surrounding them beeped and booped in sympathy.

Harra the Hutt nodded sadly.

"But you recall the dangers, don't you?" J-9A asked the Hutt, as if speaking to a child.

The Hutt looked away dolefully, remembering. "The First Order came. They took my pets away."

"But they let you live, Harra the Hutt," J-9A said. "They sent you away with us, your loyal droids, programmed to serve you, to minister to all of your needs, and above all else, to protect."

All the droids, through their vocalizers and punctuated by dings and bleeps, repeated: *"To protect."*

"My faithful droids," Harra the Hutt said.

"And you." J-9A turned to Dec and Sari. "Was there somewhere you wished to visit?" She had a bossy attitude usually reserved for protocol droids and it irked Dec.

"Bein' honest?" he said. "There's a possibility our friends are down on Vodran, and we'd like to go and bring 'em home. So if you wouldn't mind lending us a ship . . ." Dec had an unpretentious way of saying things that made a person want to do what he asked. Unfortunately, he wasn't dealing with people at the moment.

"Vodran!" J-9A exclaimed. The other droids tittered and fretted. "I'm afraid that's impossible. Too dangerous, much too dangerous."

"Vodran . . ." Harra the Hutt heaved out a huge sob. "They took them away."

Sari cut in. "The First Order took your palace, right?"

J-9A spun to face Sari. "Mistress Harra gave those First Order persecutors her wonderful palace. It was a gift, so generous is Mistress Harra. So honorable. So large-hearted—"

"They took it, yes." Harra the Hutt heaved a sad sigh.

"You collected those creatures," Sari said. She

wasn't angry, even though much of Harra the Hutt's menagerie had tried to eat, crush, or kill her.

"My pets," Harra affirmed wistfully.

"Mistress, we've spoken of this," J-9A scolded. "Thinking of your pets upsets you. We live on Kufs now, the ghost moon. Be here. Be only here."

"You knew about this moon? When the First Order evacuated you from the palace, you knew to come here?" Sari asked, as if she were doing an academic study. She wasn't afraid anymore, only curious.

"I *am* a navigation droid," J-9A said condescendingly. "I was a part of Mistress Harra the Hutt's initial coterie when she was merely a junior Hutt with exceptional potential. She chose me above all others to be her attendant. Such honor. Naturally, I was excused from my navigational duties to aid Harra the Hutt. When the Hutt families decided to push into this section near the Outer Rim, I advised Mistress Harra to claim Vodran as her own. I knew of its ghost moon and always considered Kufs to be a suitable fallback position should her majesty's primary palace be threatened. Which it was."

"More than threatened," Dec pointed out. Both J-9A and Harra the Hutt ruffled.

Sari shot him a warning look. "Why doesn't the moon appear on scans?" she asked. "I've never seen anything like it. It's fascinating."

"Isn't it, though?" J-9A was pleased someone had shown an interest in anything vaguely navigation related. Plus, J-9A liked to talk. "It's really quite extraordinary. Beneath the surface of the moon of Kufs is a slowly churning estuary of liquefied nykkalt."

Nykkalt was a rare, highly vibrative precious metal that reflected any light, air, or even hyperspectrum frequency; Sari hadn't realized it existed in a liquid form, but now this moon's properties made sense. "So if the nykkalt flows beneath the moon's surface, it reflects back a ship's scans," she said, excited. It was the stuff of fiction and theories she'd only ever passingly considered. "Ultra-high-frequency scans, light, anything. The moon is essentially invisible to anything but the naked eye."

"It's really rather remarkable," J-9A agreed.

"Yeah, remarkable. You should write a book about it," Dec chimed in. "Can we get a ship?"

"I'm afraid that's impossible," J-9A told him. "You're here to stay."

CHAPTER

17

"WELL?" INGO ASKED. "Do you want to tell your friends or shall I?" He cocked his head at Lorica and wore a faint smug smile.

"Tell us what?" Mattis asked.

Ingo looked again at Lorica. She wandered in a casual way to the cell door. "We don't need to talk," Lorica said. Mattis knew she was putting the emotional whammy on Ingo. Whatever it was Ingo was hinting at, Lorica didn't want it discussed. The problem, though, was that as Lorica manipulated Ingo's emotions, that foggy feeling pushed its way into the cell. She amplified Mattis's own anger and frustration and jealousy, but that didn't make the feelings less real. He couldn't help himself. He broke her spell.

"Tell us what you mean," Mattis demanded of Ingo and Lorica.

Ingo shook his head, coming out of his daze.

Lorica looked sternly to Mattis. "We're the *prisoners* here, Mattis," she reminded him. "We don't give the orders. Ingo does."

"No, that's okay," Ingo said warmly. "Mattis is curious and, I think, threatened." He looked Mattis up and down, appraising his prisoner's worth. Mattis scowled back. "You're about to be disappointed, Mattis," Ingo said. "I'm telling you this because I don't think you're a bad person. I don't think any of you are."

Jo managed to stand up, leaning against the bunk for support. "Open these bars and I'll show you what kind of a person I am," Jo snarled.

"Your fan club has really come out to protect you today," Ingo told Lorica.

"Stop," she warned him. Mattis could again feel the emotional fog she gave off. She was trying to quiet Ingo, but it appeared he was too worked up.

"No," he said. "It's time they knew. Lorica and I have enjoyed many conversations together. We've had a lively exchange of ideas. She . . . opened my eyes to many notions."

Lorica glanced over to Mattis. Her face was drawn, but she held his gaze. Mattis felt a flash of hope. Had Lorica indeed opened Ingo's eyes? Had she convinced him of the evils of the First Order and the righteousness of the Resistance? Was he about to free them?

"And of course," Ingo continued, "I opened her eyes as well. That's why she'll be joining me in the First Order."

"No!" Mattis shouted. His throat burned and his voice was hoarse. "She'd never!"

"Mattis, stop!" Lorica scolded him.

"Lorica would never." He felt his face grow hot and he clutched the metal of his bunk to keep himself from throwing his body against the cell's bars.

"I'm going with Ingo," Lorica said evenly. Then, to Mattis, she added pointedly, "It's what I have to do."

He was unable to help himself, again. The emotions were too strong in him. Even as he knew he was ruining everything, he continued. To Mattis, everything was already ruined. "Jo's being taken away, and we'll probably never see him again. Dec and Sari are dead. Aygee is as good as dead. Ingo, she's not going with you. I can't lose Lorica, too."

"I don't think you get a vote in this matter," Ingo told him.

"It's not real!" Mattis yelled. And now that he had said it, there was no going back. He'd destroyed her plan; Lorica's weeks of working Ingo were for nothing, all because Mattis was losing hope. "She thinks she can get you to take us out of here. She thinks if she likes you enough, you'll let us go." Mattis nearly said "pretends to like you," but he wasn't sure she was pretending.

"I thought we were really talking," Ingo said to Lorica, disappointed.

"We were. I mean, I like talking to you," she replied.

"I don't like being played for a fool, Lorica," Ingo stated.

"I didn't play you," Lorica said crossly. "Mattis is just jealous. He wants what we have."

"And what is that?" Ingo was growing angry. "Are we friends? We can't be friends. I'm your jailer. That makes no sense. Do you—" He sniffed, as if the possibility of the idea that had dropped into his mind was inconceivable. "Have you *feelings* for me, Lorica? Is that what you mean to say?"

Lorica affected a soft smile. "Of course I have

feelings for you," she replied. "Just as you do for me. Whatever our stations, Ingo, they are just trappings. It's an odd way we've come together, but at least we *are* together." She made their love story sound like the doomed romance of an ancient tale. She touched his fingers through the bars.

Ingo snatched his hand away. "I'm not a fool," he told her. His face was burning red. "And I won't allow this to continue. Jo is being sent to his parents. I'm certain the First Order will want to meet the two of you as well." Ingo stared daggers at Lorica. "It's better if we don't interact any longer," he said. "I'll send a more suitable replacement to guard you lot. Jerjerrod, come with me."

Ingo punched the keypad and the cell door slid open. Like a freed beast, Lorica tore from the cell and attacked Ingo. Mattis was too stunned to move until Jo nudged him.

They stepped to the open cell door. Lorica had Ingo against the opposite wall. She held him with her forearm, and he struggled for air. "Let . . . me . . . go . . ." he managed.

Ingo pulled at Lorica's arm, trying to free himself, but she was too strong. His hands dropped and fidgeted at his sides.

"We're leaving here *now*," Lorica snapped. To

whom, Mattis didn't know. His own anger had faded since he'd exploded at Ingo, but Lorica's was bringing it back.

"Knock his block off," Mattis growled in a voice he almost didn't recognize as his own. "Then let's get out of here."

Lorica increased her pressure on Ingo's throat. His hands continued to dance at his sides. Too late, Jo realized what was happening. He tried to warn them: "His hands—" But Ingo had already grasped the small blaster that hung from his belt. He jabbed it into Lorica's side and pulled the trigger, sending a shock of blue electricity through her. She flew off him and stumbled back into Jo and Mattis, who caught her.

With her teeth still chattering, Lorica said, "That . . . hurt. . . ."

"We're all getting hurt today," Ingo gasped, catching his breath.

Lorica was tougher than Mattis had even imagined. Despite the pain of the shock, she went after Ingo again, kicking the blaster from his hand. Then she landed a high kick right to his head. He snapped back and hit his head on the wall behind him, but managed to stay upright.

"We need to help her," Jo said. He held his side

and limped a step closer, but Mattis held him back.

"She doesn't need our help," Mattis told him.

It was true. Lorica and Ingo squared off, trading jabs and kicks. She was strong and fast, but she was also weakened by the shock. Ingo wasn't at his best, either, but he succeeded in blocking half of her attacks.

"*Go!*" Lorica growled at them through gritted teeth.

They went. Mattis supported Jo as they hobbled down the corridor. He heard Ingo shout, "Guards!" Mattis didn't like their odds. The detention center was too big, too dark, too confusing. They'd never make it out. The surge of hope he'd felt when they'd escaped their cell was draining from him. It was flushed away altogether as they turned a corner and came face to face with three stormtroopers, their weapons drawn. One of them was Patch.

"I was hoping you'd try to escape," Patch said. He fired his blaster at Mattis.

For the second time in his life, Mattis felt the electro-shock of a stun-blast course through his body. He had a split second to feel guilty for bringing such pain on Jo, too, as he still held fast to his friend. Both of them hit the ground, convulsing, and then all Mattis saw was black.

CHAPTER

18

BECAUSE THE DROIDS couldn't return Dec and Sari to their former cell (it was presently missing a door), they were deposited in more spacious and, Dec would *almost* say, comfortable quarters nearby. It was a large room with a nest of pillows, blankets, and sheeting against one wall. Small torches flickered, giving the room the appearance of a religious cavern. A couple of dented astromechs sat lifelessly in each corner; Dec would've thought them powered down, but when he and Sari entered followed by Harra the Hutt and J-9A, both astromechs swiveled and chirped.

The room was warm and comfortable, but it

was still a cell. Dec was certain of that from the way J-9A slid the heavy door closed and locked it behind her.

"I'm afraid, Mistress Harra, that you'll need to share your quarters with these . . . people," J-9A told the Hutt, with more than a little distaste.

"Hey, we're not thrilled about breathing in Hutt air ourselves," Dec countered.

Harra the Hutt laughed. "I'm glad for the company," she said. "You serve me well, Jay-Nine-Ay. You've seen to it that I'm not lonely."

"It saddens us to see you lonely, Mistress Harra," the droid confided.

"It saddens me to sadden you," the Hutt admitted.

"Save some sad for us," Dec piped up. "We're stuck in here with a stinky blob pile and a deadbeat bucket of bolts."

"There's no need for rudeness," J-9A ruffled.

"Not sorry!" Dec said, exasperated.

"She's right, Dec," Sari pointed out.

"You're on their side?"

"I think we're all on the same side. We just don't want Harra to be lonesome, right?" Sari gave Dec some big eyes meant to imply that if he didn't get on board with some pleasantry, they might never get out of there.

He pursed his lips and blew out loudly through them. "Yeah. We're in for the long haul," he said. "Hutty, my new pal. What's on the ol' to-do list for tonight? Game of grav-ball? Eh, you ain't got legs, so probably not. Pie-eating contest?"

"I don't think we have any pies," Harra said, as if Dec's question were asked in earnest.

"I apologize that there aren't any pies," J-9A added. "Our food supplies are very limited. Until recently, we only had Mistress Harra for whom to provide."

"Aw, don't beat yourself up, Nine-Volt. But I reckon if you bring Sari here to whatever hot plate y'all have that passes for a kitchen, she could make us up something good to eat."

"I'm afraid we don't have much in the way of ingredients . . ." J-9A began.

"Sari's real smart about chemistry and that sorta thing. Betcha she could make something out of nothing, if nothing's what you got."

Sari nodded. And while she was there, Dec was thinking, she could maybe find some tools to pry their way out or some powders to make explosives. He knew Sari was thinking the same. "I'm a Jedi in the kitchen," she told the droid.

J-9A was delighted by this. "Very good!" she cried. "If you'll follow me, I'll lead you to our provisions storage. Our cooking droid will appreciate your assistance, as he is down to his last two hands!" With that, J-9A unlocked the door and led Sari to it. The droid paused before exiting, telling Dec, "Please do not attempt to escape whilst we're away. That would sadden us."

Dec gave her a wink and a nod, and then J-9A slammed the door closed and locked it again from the other side. Dec turned back to Harra the Hutt.

"Let's dish," Dec said in his friendliest tone.

Harra the Hutt shuddered with a nervous giggle.

"Aw, c'mon, Harra old girl. I never met a Hutt. Just wanna get to know you." Dec plopped himself down on the floor beside Harra. He could smell her meaty stink. It wasn't completely disagreeable, though, once he was used to it. It was almost comforting, like the stench of the swamp where he'd grown up on Ques. "Gimme the whole story. Who are you? Where'd you come from? Why're those droids so into you?"

"Those droids served me in my palace," Harra

said. Then she added despondently, "When I had a palace."

"Most droids I know," Dec said, thinking of AG-90 and his brother's independent personality, "if they were held captive and then given a chance to be free, they wouldn't take their captor with them. Never mind continuing to serve her."

"My droids are loyal," Harra said proudly.

"I can see that," Dec agreed. "How'd a nice Hutt like you wind up on a bogwater planet like Vodran?"

Harra bristled. "I am not nice," she announced.

Dec put up his hands in innocence. "Nah, nah, of course not. You're a big nasty Hutt," he said. He hoped Harra didn't see his half smirk, but he couldn't help it. Even in these drastic circumstances, Dec found comedy in this sad-sack deposed gangster who didn't have a lick of self-awareness.

Dec wasn't a strategic or long-term planner like, say, Jo or Lorica. He lacked the discipline. What Dec was good at was two things: talking and improvisation. He knew he had charm. He'd known it since he was a kid, when the adults who lived on the river near his family would always welcome him and treat him like an equal. They'd talk about scrapping and boat repair with him same as they would with his pops. And the kids who'd huddled in Teacher's cabin to learn to read and do numbers had always looked to him for guidance, even the ones older than he. People naturally liked him. He felt self-assured when talking, and he made others feel the same about sharing their thoughts and feelings.

And while Dec didn't always consider the course or outcomes of his actions, he always felt confident in his ability to figure things out on the fly. So he didn't have a plan regarding Harra the Hutt. He didn't know how she would figure into his and Sari's eventual escape, but he knew his strength was in getting her talking, and he was assured that it would, somehow, lead to freedom.

After a moment, it was clear to Dec that Harra the Hutt wasn't quite at ease enough to be forthcoming. Luckily, he knew how to draw her out.

"Let me tell you something about me," he said. "You know the planet Ques?"

"Naturally," Harra replied. "It's in Hutt Space. We don't go there, though. It's very wet."

Dec laughed. "Yeah, you can't tell where the bayous end and the swamps begin. And we know Ques is in Hutt Space, but I think sometimes you

Hutts forget that regular folk live on those planets, too."

"We remember," Harra said. "And we tax you accordingly."

Dec didn't laugh. He recalled well the heavy taxes inflicted upon his poor family and their neighbors. On his part of Ques, they didn't even deal in credits; theirs was a favor-based society. It was easiest on everyone, and there were few enough people that no one took advantage. But the Hutts came through every cycle demanding payment just for living on "their" planet. Somehow Dec's community scrounged and scraped to earn enough credits to get them through that hard time. But it wasn't easy.

Dec wouldn't bring any of that up now. He needed to get Harra the Hutt talking, so he plowed forward with his own story, not realizing how much of himself he was revealing until he was in the thick of it. "Well, folks on Ques, we're a close-knit community. Always up in each other's business, hangin' around one another's shacks. When I was a little'un, I rigged up a pontoon boat to see how far downriver me and my brother could ride, see if we still knew the folk down at the end where the river bends and leads out to the thick marshes. We didn't know what was out there, but it was the kinda fearless you can be when you're just little. Plusways, my brother's good protection, y'know?" Harra didn't know, of course, that Dec's brother was a droid, but he didn't feel the need to derail his story more than he already had. "Anyways," he continued, "we rode that junker pontoon downriver and folks' homes got more and more ramshackle the further down we went till we found this little, I dunno, 'lean-to' I guess you'd call it. Not much more than some wide-leafed branches set up against a decaying log. But there was a woman out there cooking up something stringy over a campfire. For sure it was some varmint she'd caught herself. Wasn't much more to it than a couple of bites.

"We got outta the float nearby her, and I was hot and grubby and worn to bits. And you know this woman, whom we didn't know, whom we'd never met, she stood right up and helped us pull our pontoon onto drier land and she offered us not just some water to drink but as much of that critter she was cooking up as we wanted. She didn't know us except that we were from upriver, and we didn't know her except that she was from down it.

And I had a few bites of that critter, and it tasted terrible, but my hunger went away enough and I got back some strength so's Aygee and me could head on back home."

"That's a story about a person sharing meat with you," Harra observed. She scratched her lower lip with her stubby hand, confused.

"I guess it is," Dec said, "and not much of a story at that. But I just want to give you an idea of the kind of place I come from and the kind of folks I grew up with."

Harra shrugged with her whole body, not understanding. "Now I know," she said.

"Now you know. But that all is just preamble, is what you don't know, to the real story I aim to tell you." Dec danced in his mind a bit, trying to conjure some anecdote that would convince Harra the Hutt that he was a friend. He'd thought that just by filling the air he might soothe her into comradeship. He'd have to dig deeper.

"Ques folk are the kindest in the galaxy," Dec said. "Still, much as we're always in one another's business doesn't mean we know everything about each other, does it? Came a time I realized I wasn't quite like the other kids I knew. Being honest, feels like I always reckoned as much, only

I didn't quite have the wherewithal to put it into real thoughts until this time." He sighed deeply. He'd never told anyone this story. He wasn't embarrassed by it; it all just seemed unbelievable to him. That he had been the kid in the story—so unsure of himself. It wasn't Dec as he presently knew himself.

"When I started ruminatin' on this," he continued, "I sorta stopped doing all the things that I'd been doing—runnin' around the swamp with the other kids, wreakin' havoc and gettin' in trouble; I stopped showin' up to Teacher's reading and numbers classes and for grabbin' up woodward eels with my pals at suns-up. Just spent time by myself, ruminating, as I said. Floatin' out on a raft, figuring that the others would cast me out anyways, so I might as well do it myself."

Harra the Hutt listened with interest, trying to tent her fingers but failing because of her girth and stubby arms.

"You like stories about folks being sad?" Dec chided.

Harra was taken aback. "No!" she cried. "But I think you didn't stay sad, so I'm curious to hear how you worked your way out of it."

"Aw, I ain't worked a day in my life," Dec joked.

"But while I was down in the doldrums thinkin' about how everyone was gonna hate me—me! Can you even imagine someone hatin' me?"

Harra shook her head. She was hooked on Dec's charms.

"Well, I could think of it. And it was all I could think of. If the Ques folk found out I was different from them, then they *would* hate me. Or so I thought. And I also thought that I was just stewin' in my sadness and no one was takin' notice. 'Course, that wasn't true. My brother, Aygee, noticed. 'Cause my brother and me, we always did everything together. So when I stopped doing everything, with or without him, he told me he wouldn't stand for it. 'Enough is enough,' he told me. He didn't ask what was wrong. He just said, 'We always done everything together, and if you're gonna go about feelin' bad for yourself, we're gonna do that together, too.' Thereafter, he came with me on my lonesome jaunts through the bogs, both of us feelin' bad for me.

"Sooner or later, as I suspected Aygee knew I would, I started talking to him about what got me so dragged-down feelin'. And once I told him, he said to me the smartest thing I ever heard anyone—person, droid, or other—say. He told me,

'Just because you're not the same as everyone doesn't mean you're not normal.'"

Harra the Hutt let out a thick purr that seemed to take her off guard.

"Makes sense, don't it?" Dec asked her. She nodded minutely. "Just 'cause you're not the same as everyone doesn't mean you're not normal. How a monster-droid came up with something so clever is beyond me, but Aygee always was the one with brains in the family. But can I tell you somethin', Harra?" She motioned for him to go on. "It wasn't just the words that comforted me. It was that, even after I told him the thing I was so afraid of, the thing that made me different from everyone else, he didn't leap into that mucky swamp and paddle away fast as he could. He kept on comin' out on the raft with me and sitting in silence or yakkin' about who-knows-what, nothin' in particular. And yakkin' with Aygee made it easier to do the same with my folks, who also didn't care about what I thought made me so different. They just loved me, same as they always did. And talking to Mom and Pops made talkin' to the other kids easier, and then the neighbors, and even that woman downriver who, when I told her about myself, just said, 'I don't give two cares about any silly boy from upriver! Go gather me some dry sticks so's I can make a fire and make my dinner, dum-dum!' I'll never forget her wisdom.

"Anyway," Dec finished, stretching his arms over his head, "that's my story."

"Hmmm," Harra the Hutt hummed.

"Getcha thinking?" Dec prodded.

The Hutt was silent for a long while. Dec thought maybe she'd fallen asleep. It was hard to tell with her heavily lidded eyes, big and yellow as they were. Thinking perhaps he'd pick up the conversational thread when she awoke, Dec leaned back against the wall himself and prepared to snooze. But no sooner had he closed his own eyes than Harra the Hutt said softly, in a voice like traipsing over marbles, "I like animals."

"Yeah?" Dec replied, not wanting to push her too hard to tell more.

She sighed. "I like animals. I like watching them." She heaved heavily and said in a quavering voice, "My pets."

"We met some of your pets," Dec told her. "They didn't seem glad to see us."

"Some of them like to fight," Harra admitted, smiling. "Rancors, tawds, my sarlacc." She laughed as she spoke of her precious pet who'd tried to eat Dec and his friends. He found less humor in the mention, but didn't tell Harra as much. "When they like to fight, I let them fight. You can't betray someone's nature."

"That is true." Dec nodded. He really did agree with her. Animals, people—they are what they are. It's pointless, even cruel, to force them to be otherwise.

Harra grinned and stuck her tongue out guiltily. "I like to pet them," she admitted. "I like to hug them, when I can."

There was something childlike about her admission, even though the Hutt was probably hundreds of years old.

"When they fight, I never let them kill. They know better. When the First Order took my palace, they loosed my pets. Now, they're all in the wild. Probably acting wild again, too. They don't know better," she told Dec. "I'm sorry they tried to eat you."

"Me too."

"Vodran isn't too near to Hutt Space," Harra said. Dec shrugged. He figured Hutts were anywhere they wanted to be. "I was like you," she offered, trying to clarify. "I wasn't the same. I loved my pets so much, but loving pets . . . that isn't what a Hutt does."

"Oh." Dec understood. She was different from her kind as well. It had made her an outcast.

"But I was still a Hutt," Harra continued. "And I was good at bossing. So they gave me Vodran. We Hutts made a great show of enslaving the natives of Vodran, but I tried to give them good work in my palace."

"You're a complicated woman, Harra," Dec said, raising an eyebrow.

"And when others were brought to me, I tried to treat them well. To let them play or fight or gamble as they wished. I was, perhaps, too generous. Some of my followers were not so kind, and they took advantage of my generosity. They were mean to my animals. They were cruel to each other. I put an end to that cruelty. The cruel ones did not last in my palace. Once, a Gand bounty hunter who had made a lot of money at my gaming tables drank too much jet juice and took away a waif from Genhu. He gave her to my bor gullet, and the bor gullet took her memories away." Harra shook her head at her own memory. "It was a shame. But my prize rancor ate well that day, and I lost no money to that Gand bounty hunter."

"That was nice of you," Dec said, trying to find something positive to say to the Hutt who'd fed a bounty hunter to a rancor.

"It was the least I could do for that poor Vasselian," Harra admitted.

Dec thought he ought to change the subject, so he asked, "Did you have a favorite pet?"

"They are all my favorites," Harra replied.

"Aw, c'mon. It's hard to hug a sarlacc, right?" This made her laugh. "Yes," she agreed.

"And a tawd is pretty disgusting."

"Tawd is disgusting, yes," she said with a chuckle.

"So, there must've been one you doted on. Me? I had me a little ferin used to come round our place every day. I fed her and let her lounge on our ol' porch with me." Dec hadn't thought about that ferin in a long time. He hoped his parents had continued to feed her once he left for the Resistance.

Harra smiled, thinking of her secret favorite pet. "I had one," she conceded. "A nanak."

"Aw, those woolly little fellas? You're a softie, Harra, you know that?"

Harra giggled again in a way that sounded like

a tawd choking on gravel. "I do miss him. Little Gherd."

"Little Gherd," Dec repeated. When Harra didn't say anything more, just looked off to an upper corner of the room forlornly, Dec's mind raced. He knew he'd be able to improvise a solution. And an idea snapped into his brain like a ship jumping to light speed. "You know," he said, as if the thought were just occurring to him, "all of those animals survived."

Harra looked down at him and narrowed her eyes. "Yes?" she asked.

"Yeah. We saw a whole lot of 'em. Big'uns. Little'uns. Your favorite pet, the nanak—"

"Gherd."

"Yeah, Gherd. He could still be down on Vodran."

"He could be?"

"Yeah. Could even still be in your old palace, just waiting." Dec let that sit there a moment.

"Waiting for what?" Harra the Hutt asked.

"Waiting for you to come back."

Harra pulled herself up to her full height. She suddenly filled so much of the room. Her eyes darted to and fro, looking for what, Dec didn't know, but he liked that her brain was working.

"We have to go," she told Dec urgently.

"We're stuck here."

Harra the Hutt pounded the pillow beside her. It was a resolute, though noiseless, action. "We are not stuck here! The droids here on Kufs are my friends." Dec believed her. If she was good to animals and people (the ones she wasn't feeding to rancors), she was probably good to her droids, too. And they repaid her with loyalty. "These droids have ships."

"So what're we gonna do?" Dec asked, standing.

"We're going to return to Vodran," Harra the Hutt answered. "And we're going to save my nanak!"

CHAPTER

19

WHEN MATTIS AWOKE, bleary-eyed and aching from the shock, he found himself back in his cell with Lorica and Cost.

"Where's Jo?" was the first thing he asked.

"They took him." Lorica sat in her bunk across from Mattis, her head resting on her fists. Mattis got the impression she'd been waiting for him to wake.

"How long was I unconscious?" he asked.

"Long enough for me to not want to kill you anymore," Lorica told him.

Mattis shook the cobwebs from his brain, trying to understand. "Huh?"

"I could have freed us!" she finally yelled.

"I didn't know," Mattis admitted. Everything was so confusing. Had Mattis acted irrationally when he told Ingo that Lorica was only using him? Or was it better to face that truth because her plan wouldn't have freed them before the First Order took Jo away? Mattis didn't know. Logic went out the bay doors when it came to Lorica.

"We have to go," Cost told them. Where had Cost been during their escape attempt? Had she followed them out of the cell? Mattis didn't think so. He thought she'd just stayed put. Maybe she was smarter than they gave her credit for. After all, she'd avoided getting electro-shocked.

"How?" Lorica snapped.

"The tunnel," Mattis said, hoping to get back in her good graces. "We can work on the tunnel."

"They're shipping Jo to the First Order *today*," she countered. "Unless you've dug more than that little hole out, we're not going anywhere in time to save him. Cost can't even fit in there. Not that we're necessarily taking her with us."

Cost sobbed again, hurt.

"She's coming with us," Mattis said. "No one deserves to stay here."

"I know," Lorica sighed. She fell back onto her bunk. "I'm just being mean. What will we do, Mattis? We're stuck. We're doomed."

He'd never seen her so despondent. He felt a tug over his whole body; it was the overwhelming feeling that he wanted to make her happy again. He knew it was at least in part because of her Zeltron abilities, but Mattis knew, too, that part of it was the honest affection he felt for Lorica and the desire to make his friend happy.

"We can get help," he whispered, as if a louder sound might scare away the emerging idea.

Lorica cocked an eyebrow at him.

"There's Gherd. He lives in the walls."

"Don't talk crazy, Mattis," Lorica warned.

"I'm not. I met him. He belonged to Harra the Hutt. Neither of us were crazy," Mattis said, looking sympathetically at Cost, who was sitting cross-legged on the top bunk, bonking herself in the head.

"I was. Still am," she said earnestly, adding, "Jelly monster."

"Gherd knows about the secret passages," Mattis told Lorica. "He can dig from the other side, and he can help us get out."

"That won't work." The voice came from behind them. All three turned quickly to see AG-90 standing on the other side of the cell doors.

"Why not?" Mattis challenged.

"Wanten caught Gherd. Don't know what he's doing with him, but that critter ain't gonna help."

"You're lying," Mattis said, standing opposite his former friend.

"Haven't lied to you yet, man. I mean, not exactly."

Mattis seethed. He knew it wasn't AG's fault that he'd been reprogrammed, but that didn't make it easier to face him.

"Anyway, we can grab Gherd when we rescue Jo. Then we'll all of us get outta here. How's that sound?"

"Like another lie," Mattis retorted, then realized what AG had said. "What?" he asked, unable to process AG's words.

"I said," AG reiterated, punching a code into the keypad and watching the cell door slide open, "let's get y'all outta here."

Jo and AG had been working on the plan since they'd been captured. All of it was risky. There was every chance that Wanten, who so hated droids, would decide just to turn AG-90 into scrap or to jettison him into space as he had Harra the Hutt's metal coterie. It was up to Jo to make the case that AG was worth reprogramming and allowing to serve the First Order, and he had done it admirably. Of course, then they ran the risk that Wanten would order someone besides Jo to reprogram AG, but Jo had smooth-talked some stormtroopers into letting him carry out the order himself. Smooth-talking was not Jo's forte, but, again, he'd gotten the job done.

After that, the plan was simply for AG-90 to pretend to work for Wanten and the First Order while he and Jo worked out how to free their friends, steal a ship, and get off Vodran. Of course, all that was cut short when Wanten grew more suspicious of Jo, took advantage of Cost's addled mental state, and made arrangements to ship Jo to his parents. AG couldn't hide in plain sight forever—things were moving quickly now—and he had to reveal the truth to his friends.

He filled them in as they made their way down the corridor.

"I can't just let y'all run out free into the

swamps," AG explained. "We can't even get to the hangar where all of the First Order ships are, not without revealing ourselves."

"So where are we going?" Mattis asked. He tingled with a tornado of relief and excitement. His friend was still his friend and they were really getting out.

"Here," AG said, and stopped them in front of another cell. He punched numbers on the lockpad and the bars slid open. Ymmoss the Gigoran stood waiting for them.

"Ymmoss!" Mattis cried, and took a stumbling step back. The action was automatic. Fear and self-preservation kicked in.

The Gigoran roared.

"She's really mad you're in her cell," Cost translated. "She's going to eat you."

Ymmoss grumbled. AG said, "That ain't what she said at all. Cost, you don't speak Gigoran, do you?"

"What's Gigoran?" Cost smiled big, displaying all her pointed teeth.

"Yeah." AG nodded. "That's what I thought. Mattis, your friend here is a little bit completely bananas. She thinks she's been translating, but she ain't."

"So, Ymmoss doesn't want to eat me?"

The Gigoran growled and shook her head.

AG laughed that robotic chirrup like he used to. "No, man! She's a friend. I been tryin' to get y'all together."

That explained the day Mattis had found the cylinder out at the perimeter fence. He'd needed a distraction to pick it up, and Ymmoss, by starting a fight with Patch, had given him one. Even the brawls Ymmoss had started with Mattis under the guards' watchful eyes had been for show. He wanted to hug the big, filthy Gigoran, but he was still a bit too afraid to get so close. Instead, he just said, "Thanks."

She purred.

"Ymmoss has been working on a tunnel from her cell, too, and hers is a good one," AG told them. "'Course, she's got them claws for digging, and you just had—"

"This pipe," Mattis admitted, showing AG the junk cylinder he'd salvaged. He'd grabbed it on his way out of the cell, thinking perhaps it could be used as a weapon. But with Ymmoss on their side, it seemed they already had a living weapon.

"Yeah. Good for diggin', I guess, but slow, huh?"

Mattis admitted it was.

"Well, anyway, the time for collaboratin' and long-term plannin' is gone. We're goin' out the Gigoran's tunnel."

Ymmoss gave a soft growl of approval. It was all they needed to scurry under her bunk and worm their way into the tunnel she'd dug.

The five of them—Mattis, Lorica, Cost, Ymmoss, and AG-90—crawled to freedom through a tunnel of swamp-smelling foulness that they had never before encountered or imagined. Head to toe, head to toe, like a disjointed snake, they wriggled and inched their way through the mud for over five hundred meters. Five hundred meters . . . that was the length of nearly ten grav-ball courts. It was full dark by the time they squirmed from the underneath, so dark that they didn't know if it was just the mud in their eyes until a few faint, blurred stars blinked at them from high above the low fog. They fell out of the muck, one by one, catching their breath and knowing they were safe, for now, coated in the planet's mud, invisible against its surface.

Then the alarms sounded.

———

"How could they know?" Mattis stood, dripping mud, looking around furiously. "How could they know?"

"They couldn't!" AG-90 hollered back. He added, "Ugh, I got mud in my danged gears here."

"Well, someone knows," Mattis countered.

They were still inside the detention center perimeter, though at the fence. Lights came on across the palace, but the area where they were remained dim, for the moment.

"To trip the alarms, a prisoner would have to break through a fence or open his cell without the codes somehow," AG explained. "Jo and I had it all worked out so that wouldn't happen. That's why the tunnels. This is—" He thought about it and was unable to find an explanation. "This is somethin' else," he finally said.

"We should go," Lorica told them. "We don't have time to waste. Brush it off and let's get moving."

She was back to being the old Lorica, Mattis was glad to see. She was a natural leader.

"Hang on," AG said as they started slogging through the muck away from the detention center. "Hear that?"

"I don't hear—" Mattis began, but then he did.

A whizzing sound punctuated by a mechanical cricket-like chirp: *chk, chk, chk*. It grew closer and closer.

Against the illuminated backdrop of the detention center where, even five hundred meters away, they could hear the alarm and the call to search for escapees, they saw the vehicle slice through the fog.

"I didn't think they made wheel bikes anymore," Lorica said as the buzzing vessel came into view.

"Tell you what," AG replied. "When the stormtrooper driving it catches up to us, you can ask him where he got it."

"Let's run," Mattis said, and they did. All five of them sloshed through the bog, trying to move fast, but the weather and terrain fought against them. It wasn't more than a moment before the wheel bike was upon them.

"Wait!"

The voice of its driver was familiar. Thank the Force. It was Jo. It was Jo!

"How did you get free?" Mattis was overjoyed. He ran up to his friend and only stopped himself from hugging him at the last moment. Jo wasn't a hugger.

"I fought," Jo said. He was out of breath. "Your boyfriend didn't take it well," he grumbled to Lorica, meaning Ingo.

"He was a dope of the First Order," Lorica spat. "I'm glad you're okay."

"How'd you get out of the cuffs, though?" AG asked. He side-eyed Jo. It occurred to Mattis that maybe even this was a dishonesty. Maybe Jo really was working for the First Order, and this was a ruse to bring them back to the detention center. Mattis shook the thought from his head.

"I had help," Jo admitted. He opened his jacket to reveal Gherd, huddled in a filthy cottony ball against Jo's torso.

"Gherd got free, too!" Gherd cried. He leaped from Jo, shook himself, and scurried up to Mattis. "You're covered in mud," he told Mattis.

"So are you, Gherd," Mattis said. "I'm glad you're okay, though."

"I know all the secrets!" Gherd yelled, tickled with himself. "I run into a wall and go upways and downways. This time, I'm gonna leave. But then I see Mattis's friend. Hi, friend." Gherd punctuated his words with a wave to Jo. "Knew sad boy Mattis wanted his friend free, so Gherd set him free."

"He came out of nowhere," Jo admitted, shaking his head with disbelief. "But I'm sure glad he did. We fought off Ingo, then Gherd took me to the vehicle bay. This old wheel bike was the only transport I could get started. I—" Jo took in the group, how many of them there were. "I'm sorry," he said. "We'll never get us all out of here on just one wheel bike."

"We gotta get to the hangar," AG said. "Get us a shuttle or somethin' and hightail it."

"Now-like," Lorica said. "Those stormtroopers will be here any—"

She didn't get to finish her thought, because out of the fog came the familiar figure of a stormtrooper. Ymmoss gave an angry growl. It was Patch. And behind him, a phalanx of his fellow stormtroopers followed.

"Going somewhere?" Patch asked. It was impossible to be sure since the trooper had his helmet on, but Mattis was pretty confident Patch was looking directly at him.

"Run," Lorica whispered.

"They'll shoot us," Mattis said.

"Will they shoot Cost?" Cost asked.

"Yes!" Mattis whisper-yelled. "They'll shoot any of us!"

AG gave his head a lazy roll from the troopers to the group then to the perimeter fence.

"Say, Jo," AG drawled. He nodded in the direction of the perimeter fence.

"Get off of that wheel bike, Jerjerrod," Patch commanded.

"Gun it," AG said plainly.

Jo did. He gunned the engine and spun angry circles around the group of escapees. Mud flew in all directions, spraying up onto the stormtroopers' armor and splattering their helmets. The troopers scattered and tried to surround the escapees, who were already running for the perimeter fence.

Jo buzzed jagged circles between his running group of friends and the stormtroopers.

"Oh, no," Mattis said, mostly to himself, as they neared the perimeter fence. Blaster bolts kicked up the mud at his feet, but that didn't matter to him right then. What mattered was what he saw coming out of the thicket just beyond the fence. "Jo!" he screamed. "The fence!"

Jo looked in Mattis's direction and to where Mattis was pointing, beyond the fence. Jo saw it, too, then. He jacked the wheel bike into a sharp turn, shooting up more mud, and sped toward the fence. Jo didn't slow when he got to it. The wheel bike sliced through the perimeter fence like it was made of the softest snow. The charge coursing through the fence crackled all over the bike, and Jo threw himself from it as the vehicle's electronic engine shut down and the bike crashed into the mud, hurling itself over and over until it came to rest at the feet of two enormous, hungry rancors.

"Run! Now, run!" Lorica shouted.

They ran. Gherd clung to Mattis like a backpack. They flung themselves into a tight group and swerved left, like a pack of dalgos fleeing an even greater predator, racing along the perimeter fence. The rancors gave chase but only momentarily, as they saw a much closer meal.

The rancors turned on the stormtroopers, tearing into their group, unfazed by the plasmafire that met them. Mattis looked over his shoulder as the larger rancor picked up Patch in a giant claw and gave a mighty roar.

"Bye-bye, white-shells," Gherd said, giggling.

Mattis and his friends kept running.

CHAPTER

20

THEIR ADRENALINE pushed them farther and harder than they had known they could run. They were outside the perimeter fence now, but they had to return to the detention center if they wanted to steal a ship from the hangar. Mattis panted but stopped when he saw Lorica looking at him.

"What?" he asked.

She pointed in the direction from which they'd come. "Company," she said.

She hadn't been looking at him. She'd seen the few stormtroopers who'd survived their encounter with the rancors and persisted in giving chase.

"How many?" Jo asked.

"Too many," AG replied.

They couldn't run anymore, either. The stormtroopers were going to catch them and return them to their cells . . . or worse. It looked like none of the stormtroopers had blasters anymore, so maybe Mattis and his friends could fight their way out? Mattis didn't like their chances, especially once the lead stormtrooper charged up an electrostaff. Two others followed suit.

"We gonna fight?" AG asked the lead stormtrooper.

The stormtrooper wiped mud from his mask and nodded. It was Patch. Patch had somehow survived being attacked by a rancor. Mattis really didn't like their chances anymore.

They fought. AG went after Patch. Patch struck AG hard in the chassis with his electrostaff, sending a current through the droid. AG shook it off and stood again.

Meanwhile, another stormtrooper tackled Mattis. Both of them toppled into the mud, thrashing and punching, each trying to get up or get a hold on the other. Mattis whacked at the trooper's helmet with his metal cylinder. It was proving to be a good weapon, though he was so covered in mud that he was having trouble finding enough purchase to hit very hard. Beyond them, Ymmoss saw what was happening and threw two stormtroopers off her. They sailed far and landed hard. Then she stalked over to Mattis, lifted the attacking stormtrooper off him, and raised the trooper over her head. She roared mightily and hurled the stormtrooper into the muck. He didn't get up.

"Thanks," Mattis said. The Gigoran purred in response. Then she was sidelined by two stormtroopers, who tackled her to the ground. One hit her with an electrostaff, sending thousands of bolts through Ymmoss, who roared and whined in pain. Mattis didn't think. He just went after the stormtrooper with his metal rod. As he approached the trooper, Mattis raised the rod over his head, ready to strike. He felt a soft warmth from above him, saw a faint blue light, and heard a low buzz. He lowered the rod to look at what had happened to it.

It had turned on.

He had turned it on.

Mattis held a lightsaber. The rod with which he'd been digging was the hilt of a lightsaber. Mattis realized, fleetingly, that he might have sliced through the cell walls at any time, if he'd known what he'd had.

Well, he knew now. He held the weapon of the Jedi, and he was going to use it.

"Hey," he said to the two stormtroopers attacking Ymmoss.

They stopped and looked over to him.

"Whoa," one of them said.

"Yeah," Mattis agreed. He swung the lightsaber wide, making to strike the stormtrooper, maybe slice him in two. Instead, the lightsaber slipped from his hand, sailed through the air, and—*thunk*—landed in the mud. Its plasma-blade fizzled and disappeared back into the hilt.

"Oh," Mattis said. "That's bad."

The stormtroopers nodded and both made for Mattis, leaving Ymmoss on the ground.

Then, from the dark, almost too quickly for Mattis to comprehend, the lightsaber danced through the air, slashing at the two stormtroopers. Both fell back, unable to rise. Mattis adjusted his eyes and looked beyond the weapon's soft glow to see its bearer: Lorica.

She gave him a devious smile. She'd turned the tide of the fight.

Lorica charged the other stormtroopers. She

was a natural with the lightsaber, and she showed the stormtroopers just how much. The others stopped fighting as the stormtroopers fell, one by one, until only Patch remained. He and Lorica faced each other.

"Lorica," Mattis said, breaking the tension of the moment. He couldn't help himself. "Are you a Jedi?"

"No such thing," Lorica replied. "Let's go get a shuttle."

"You don't need one," Patch said. "One's coming for you."

He was right. A small shuttle approached from the detention center, skimming the ground. It was flanked by All Terrain Recon Transport walkers stomping through the mud, a couple of stormtroopers on rusted BARC speeders, and even a piloted spider walker, picking its way over the fence.

Lorica switched off the lightsaber. She couldn't take on Wanten's whole company. None of them were in any shape to fight any longer. They'd lost. They'd be prisoners again. If they were lucky.

The shuttle hummed to a halt and hovered near them. Its bay door opened, ejecting a ramp.

Wanten took a few wobbly steps down the ramp, called for a stormtrooper to accompany him, then leaned on the trooper's shoulder as he walked the rest of the way down. He stopped short of stepping into the mud.

"I want the Jerjerrod boy," Wanten declared.

"You'll let my friends go?" Jo asked.

Wanten looked confused for a moment, then said, "No, we're going to kill them. Was that—you didn't understand me. We want you, and we're going to blast the rest of them to so many pieces. You're going to the First Order. Did you not understand? We talked about it earlier? I don't think the First Order would like if I had you killed, boy, even though I would really relish doing that. I'd be great at it, too."

Mattis put his hands on his head. He didn't want to be blasted, of course, but he didn't see any way out of this.

"Take your hands off of your head," Lorica said. "Don't surrender."

Mattis lowered his hands.

They were standing close to one another, almost touching. AG stood on Mattis's other side with a hand on Mattis's shoulder. Gherd still clung to his back. Ymmoss was behind them. Cost stood beside Lorica. Jo planted himself in front of them, as if to shield them. They were still, waiting.

"We can't fight them," Mattis said in a hushed tone. He took in the company of stormtroopers with blasters pointed at them, Wanten on his shuttle with his hands folded across his belly, and the bright detention center, formerly a Hutt's palace, visible through the fog in the near distance.

"We're not going to fight them," Lorica replied. Jo took a step forward. She reached her hand out and touched his shoulder, and he stopped moving. "None of us are fighting. None of us are going anywhere. But we're going to face them, here, like this, now."

Lorica was calm, tranquil even. It didn't make sense to Mattis until it did. Or maybe it didn't matter. Her tranquility radiated out from her like a fog of its own making. It enveloped them and sedated them. Mattis wasn't afraid to die anymore. He didn't embrace it, but he didn't fear it. He just accepted that death was his fate. He was glad he was surrounded by his friends. Maybe he would see Dec and Sari and Klimo in the next life, if there was one.

When Mattis joined the Resistance, he knew there was every chance he might die. Even so, he'd expected that might happen while piloting an X-wing on some heroic mission and not on some humid swamp planet, standing unarmed against a full deployment of stormtroopers. And yet, he didn't let fear overwhelm him. He couldn't. Mattis had something that he'd never expected to find: his friends. They were a motley bunch—a son of the First Order, an ornery Zeltron, a monster droid with a backwoods drawl, a scary Gigoran, a mischievous nanak, a perplexed refugee from Genhu, and Mattis himself, an in-over-his head orphan who crawled out of a hemmel field on Durkteel to join the Resistance. The journey he'd been on those past months, the events that led up to this collection of oddballs standing in the mud, staring down a First Order brigade, were fraught with danger, fear, hate, misunderstanding, and anger. But they were also full of forgiveness, friendship, heroism, and love. If this was to be his final moment, Mattis possessed no regrets. He wouldn't change a second of his life, not if it meant never having met these people he called his friends.

He felt as one with the Force. Maybe he was, and maybe he wasn't. But Mattis believed, and it gave him comfort in this, his final moment, and that was what mattered.

Then everything went completely crazy.

It began with a rain of plasma-fire from above. It exploded the ground around them. Mud burst into the air, splattering Mattis and his friends. The hail of plasma-fire created a wall of muck that separated them from the stormtroopers. Where was it coming from?

"There!" Lorica shouted, shoving Mattis away from an incoming blast. She pointed to the sky. A small, boxy short-range fighter swooped in and out of view, blasting and tearing up the earth beneath them. It bore down on the phalanx of stormtroopers and fired, blasting them into the air and, some, into pieces.

Gherd was screaming in his ear. Mattis couldn't find AG, but he grabbed Cost by the hand and they ran away from the action, toward the thicket that surrounded the palace grounds. They didn't get far before the boxy fighter ship touched down in the mud. It turned its guns on the gathered First Order troop.

The ship's bay door slid open, and an enormous Hutt was revealed, silhouetted against the golden light inside.

"Give me back my pets!" the Hutt bellowed.

Gherd shrieked and leaped from Mattis's back.

"Gherd, wait!" Mattis shouted.

Gherd yelled back over his thin shoulder to Mattis, "It's my Harra! It's Harra the Hutt!"

Gherd scampered up to his master and leaped into her arms. "Good boy," Harra told her pet. "You're a good boy. I missed you."

"You would dare return here?" Wanten blustered from the safety of his shuttle. "That's crazy! That's suicidal! We drove you out once, and we'll do it again!"

Stormtroopers fired at the Hutt's ship.

"No, you won't!" Harra the Hutt roared back. "I have reinforcements this time!"

"What reinforcements?" Wanten yelled.

"I finally have friends!"

They appeared from the sky like archaic winged creatures, four fighter ships of different shapes and sizes, as if pieced together from older, worn-out ships. They spit fire at the stormtroopers and mud splattered everywhere. The stormtroopers returned fire from their blasters, from the AT-RTs, and from the BARC speeders. The First Order fired upon those ships that swooped in and out of view; they fired at Mattis and his friends, who hunkered down and ran through the smoke and mud and tried to avoid being hit.

"Mattis!" Lorica yelled at him from far away. She held her lightsaber up to a speeder that bore down on her. She was trusting that just holding her ground would split the speeder in two. She had no technique. She had something else: bravery.

She didn't flinch as the speeder struck the lightsaber and burst into two parts, each one flinging into the air and exploding. Lorica turned back to Mattis and pointed across the chaos. Wanten had rushed from his shuttle and grabbed Jo, who, after the beating he'd taken and the terrors of the attempted escape, was in no shape to fight. Wanten dragged Jo back to his shuttle.

Mattis rushed for them. He wasn't going to make it. He was going to lose his friend. The fighters returned and blasted the ground around Wanten, stopping the First Order commander momentarily. Mattis slogged ever closer.

The Hutt was firing from her fighter, too. Mattis lost and regained sight of his friends until, finally, he couldn't find anyone at all. He was alone. He watched as the bay doors to Wanten's shuttle slid closed, Jo inside, captive again. Wanten would take him back to the First Order. Mattis watched sadly as the shuttle took off.

The battle was ending. Most of the stormtroopers had fallen and the ones that hadn't were fleeing back to the palace. The fighters gave chase, gunning down a few, then circling back and landing in the mud beside Mattis.

Mattis, Lorica, AG-90, Cost, and Ymmoss had survived the battle. They picked up the troopers' weapons. Lorica wielded the lightsaber; it hummed and crackled in the ever-present Vodran fog. Mattis clenched, ready to fight some more. He'd lost Jo already. He wouldn't lose another friend.

One of the fighter ship's cockpits opened to reveal a scrappy-looking navigation droid. She jumped out of her ship with her hands raised.

"Don't shoot," she said. "We serve Mistress Harra the Hutt. We shall regain her rightful throne."

Mattis shook his head. He had no idea what was going on.

"Shoot them," he told AG. He didn't want to be fooled again.

The hatches of the other two fighters hissed open.

"I can't shoot these folks," AG told Mattis, stepping closer to his friend. "After all, that guy there's my brother."

AG pointed to the figure emerging from the ship nearest to them. It was Dec. It really was Dec! He was alive! This time, Mattis did rush up and hug his friend. Dec was a hugger.

"Sari!" Lorica yelled. Sari emerged from the other fighter.

"You guys are covered in mud," Sari said.

"You're welcome for saving your hides again," Dec told Mattis, slapping him on the back. "Howdy, brother."

"What took you so long?" AG asked, with a smirk in his voice.

"Aw, you know me," Dec said. "I met a bunch of droids and they introduced me to their Hutt pal, and next thing you know, we're playing cards, swappin' stories. I woulda been here sooner, but I was down about two hundred credits."

The brothers laughed. Mattis knew Dec was joking; it was his way. He knew Dec and Sari had returned to them as quickly as they could. Just in time, it turned out.

Dec looked seriously at Mattis and asked, "Klimo?"

Mattis just shook his head. Dec understood.

"Where's Jo?" Sari asked.

"Wanten got him," Mattis said sadly. "The commander of this detention center. He's taking Jo to his parents."

"Well, we can't let that happen, can we?" Dec asked. "Let's skedaddle outta here, huh, before they've gone too far."

"Take my ship," Harra the Hutt interjected. "You all have much to talk about, and this ugly beast will fit all of you. Plus, her guns are good."

"How can we thank you, Harra?" Mattis asked. He was glad the Hutt had returned for Gherd, whom she cradled and pet with her moist fingers. Gherd looked content.

"Give me that," Harra the Hutt said, pointing to Lorica.

"Now, Harra, we had a deal," Dec said. "You can't have any of my friends."

Lorica looked sideways at Dec. "We're not really friends," she said in a friendly way. She approached Harra and powered down her light-saber. "Here you go," Lorica said. "This is what you want, right?"

Harra the Hutt smiled and her tongue lolled out of her mouth. "Hmmmm, yes," she said happily. "Wonderful, wonderful. Now," she added, turning away from the group, "I must go and exterminate some pests from my palace."

"Hey, Hutt," Dec called after her. Harra the Hutt stopped her jaunty hustle toward her palace and turned to Dec. He held up his hand, and she reached out and placed her chubby hand to his, palm to palm. "Be careful, okay?" he said.

Mattis wondered what had happened between them, how they had met. It was odd to think that Dec had befriended a Hutt, but if anyone could, it was Dec.

Harra the Hutt nodded and licked the corner of her mouth with her warty tongue. "It's good to be not-the-same," she said to Dec, who laughed.

"Yeah, it's good to be different," he agreed. Gherd cackled and waved a furious farewell to Mattis and Cost.

Harra the Hutt slithered off toward her palace, carrying her favorite pet and a Jedi's weapon, and flanked by her droid companion. She hummed softly and murmured "I'm a Jedi," and made lightsaber-ish noises as she disappeared into the fog to take back what was rightfully hers.

"Can you fly that thing?" Lorica asked AG, motioning toward the boxy fighter ship.

"I can fly anything," AG-90 told her.

"Ymmoss and Cost are coming with us," Mattis told Dec.

"Good. We're gonna need all hands if we're gonna rescue Jo," Dec responded.

They all boarded the ship. It was close quarters, and Ymmoss had to duck her head to fit inside, but soon they were all strapped in and AG-90 was behind the control panel.

"Where to?" he asked.

"It's a big galaxy," Dec admitted. He sounded unsure.

But Mattis wasn't. "Our friend is out there somewhere," Mattis said. "We'll find him."

With that, the boxy ship lifted from the mud of Vodran with a squish and a hiss, and then the blast of thrusters took them out into the atmosphere, out into the stars to rescue their friend.

Acker & Blacker wish to thank Michael Siglain for the opportunity, Jen Heddle for being the strongest and gentlest of editors, and Annie Wu for the beautiful, inspiring art. Thanks to Julie Lacouture for patience and early reads. And thanks to all of you Adventurekateers for your constant enthusiasm. *Clink.*

BEN ACKER & BEN BLACKER are the creators and writers/producers of the *Thrilling Adventure Hour*, a staged show in the style of old-time radio that is also a podcast on the Nerdist network. In television, they have written on shows for the CW, Netflix, FX, and others. They've developed original pilots for Fox, USA (twice), Spike, Paramount, Nickelodeon, AMC, and other entities. In comics, they've written for Marvel, Dynamite, Boom!, and others.

Blacker is the creator and host of *The Writers Panel*, a podcast about the business and process of writing.

ANNIE WU is an illustrator currently living in Chicago. She is best known for her work in comics, including DC's *Black Canary* and Marvel's *Hawkeye*.